THE
ETERNAL
OPTIMIST
It's Never Too Late

Matt Drinkhahn

MVH.

Creative contribution by Lisa Shiroff
Cover Design & Book Layout - DBree, StoneBear Design

Manufactured and printed in the United States of America distributed globally by markvictorhansenlibrary.com
New York | Los Angeles | London | Sydney

ISBN: 979-8-88581-148-4 Hardback
ISBN: 979-8-88581-149-1 Paperback
ISBN: 979-8-88581-150-7 eBook
Library of Congress Control Number: 2024903306

Testimonials

"An uplifting masterpiece that radiates positivity and inspires hope. *The Eternal Optimist* is a heartfelt journey through the power of optimism, resilience, and the unwavering belief in a brighter tomorrow. In a world filled with challenges, this book serves as a beacon of light, reminding us that a positive mindset can transform our lives. A must-read for anyone seeking motivation, encouragement, and a renewed sense of optimism"

— **Justin Donald**, #1 *WSJ* and *USA Today* Best-Selling Author, Founder of The Lifestyle Investor, Host of The Lifestyle Investor Podcast

"When it comes to practicing what one preaches and truly living as an eternal optimist, look no further than Matt Drinkhahn. He IS this book. He owns his mistakes and learns from them. Anyone who reads this would do well to look for the transformation when the main character goes from selfish to selfless, from ego-driven to emotionally available for those around him, from perfectionist to at-peace. This man is making a difference in the world, and I cannot recommend him enough."

— **Phillip Stutts**, Author, *The Undefeated Marketing System*

"Matt Drinkhahn's *The Eternal Optimist* explores the mindset of a man who makes a lot of mistakes and then, through curiosity, finally solves the puzzle of connecting with others. I've observed that when people remain curious, their potential is limitless. Even in difficulty, there are chances to enhance strengths through the power of observation. My friendship and professional experiences with Matt are rooted in our shared values including gratitude, optimism, and resilience in the face of challenges. These

themes and lessons are beautifully threaded throughout his book, and it is a must-read for anyone who has experienced a pattern of repeating mistakes and is ready to get unstuck and uplifted."

—**Amber Vilhauer**, CEO and Founder, NGNG Enterprises

"Optimism can be our most powerful mindset, but it can also become our biggest blind spot if we use it to avoid the deep realities of life. In this powerful story, master mindset coach Matt Drinkhahn demonstrates how we can harness our optimism to live not just a successful life but a whole life, and why wholeness is the greatest success of all. I recommend it to any entrepreneur who wants to put their most powerful mindset to work for them rather than against them."

— **Dr. Kelly Flanagan**, Author/Speaker/Coach/Psychologist

"Matt is a friend, a peer, and an inspiration as an eternal optimist! As one who has learned and grown through my mistakes, adversity, and challenges, I know that mindset and maintaining a positive attitude are everything. Matt exemplifies this in his resilience, integrity, curiosity, authenticity, and optimism, as depicted in his work and the stories in his book. This book is for anyone who needs an extra dose of empowerment, encouragement, and hope in their business and life."

— **Julie Reisler**, Transformation Expert, The You-est You® Podcast Host, Author, Georgetown University Professor
juliereisler.com

"If you keep doing what you have always done, you will keep getting what you have always gotten. It is so easy to point out mistakes others make and so hard to see them in ourselves. In this

incredible book Matt takes a journey through life. His persistence and optimism keep him going despite his many setbacks. Just like the real-life Matt who has touched so many of us through his friendship and his podcasts you will see that it is not what happens to you that counts. It is how you react to it. Pick up a copy today. Give another to your friends when they need some optimism in their lives. And never forget to make the world a better place!"

— **Eric Wohlwend**, #1 Best-selling Author of *Family Success Triangle* and Host of Real Power Family Radio Show

"The thing I most love about Matt Drinkhahn is that he writes about his own experience and teaches others from the lessons he has learned himself. He uses his own experience of adversity and challenge to teach others how to grow and to see their mistakes as gifts that forward their journey through life toward success. The reader will benefit from his stories and his insights and come out the better person for it."

— **Marcia Martin**, Renowned International Executive Trainer and Life Coach, marciamartin.com

"Matt weaves a tale with such elegance and grace that I found myself deeply moved, hurting, and cheering for the hero of the story and his family. I don't believe you can read *The Eternal Optimist* and not be affected by it as it challenges you to look at your own relationships, biases, and assumptions. I am hopeful all readers come out a little stronger and more grounded upon completion."

— **Eric Farewell**, CEO & Founder, Aviator Paramotor

"My family and I are inspired by the optimism that Matt brings forth every day. I've had the honor of calling him an inspiration,

motivator, and incredible friend for the last four years after we met in Front Row Dads. My wife and I look forward to school mornings and hearing the inspiring words, stories, and inspiration that he shares on his Instagram lives, and we both enjoy his podcasts as he digs in deeper with other optimists in the world. The world is a better place when we have talented people spreading optimism, especially Matt Drinkhahn."

— **Jason Bronstad**, Husband, Front Row Dad, & CEO of MALK Organics

"Since I met Matt at a live event, I saw a man who values lifelong learning, curiosity, and practicing what he preaches. He's intentional and takes action when it comes to his strategy for growth. This book offers a glimpse into the thinking that has helped him to find inner peace and impact so many. Stay curious and read this to learn how!"

- **Tony DiLorenzo** — Best Selling Author of *The 6 Pillars of Intimacy*® and Co-Host of the ONE Extraordinary Marriage Show

"This book is an essential companion for those navigating life's toughest challenges. In my personal journey of overcoming cancer at twenty-five, I've witnessed the transformative power of trusting that things are working in your favor, even in the darkest moments. Matt's remarkable ability to inspire hope and resilience serves as a priceless source of encouragement for anyone in need and is a testament to the strength within us all."

– **Courtney Elmer**, Globally-Ranked Host, *Insider Secrets to a Top 100 Podcast, The EffortLESS Life*®

"Matt is one of the most ambitious, optimistic and grounded people I know. As a fellow entrepreneur, I've dealt with plenty of adversity, and I know I can turn to Matt for both wisdom and real-life examples of overcoming challenges and emerging better for it. I highly recommend this book!"

– **Dustin Riechmann**, Founder of 7FigureLeap.com

"When I first met Matt, I loved the fact that he is upfront about being an optimist. I am often accused of being an optimist like it is a bad thing, naive, unrealistic, when it is the complete opposite. So, I knew I was in good company with him, and we clicked straight away. Then I heard his story and was in awe of where his optimism springs from. He is so inspirational, that to learn he had put his wisdom into a book I was thrilled to be able to get my hands on it. I cannot thank him enough for creating the podcast and writing this book to spread the word that our world needs, so that we can change and rediscover what it means to lead with your heart and remain positive about all our futures. We all need to be more Matt!"

— **Gill Tiney**, Founder of Collaboration Global

"Life challenges you and forces you to failure. It's not a walk in the park. Matt's (this story) illustrates that and how when one keeps learning through failure, they can succeed. Thoroughly recommend you walk towards the pain and read Matt's book."

— **Thomas Power**, Co-Founder BIP100 Club

"A captivating book that mirrors the author's engaging personality. Much like Matt himself, *The Eternal Optimist* effortlessly draws readers in, keeping them hooked and eager for more. I literally

could not stop reading. Through a seamless blend of wisdom and a sophisticated yet enjoyable writing style, Drinkhahn imparts valuable insights that make this book informative and delightful. The ultimate combination."

— **Rodric Lenhart** - Author of *Million Dollar Flip Flops*, Speaker, Coach, World Wanderer

"An engaging story. Coach Matt brings to life the challenges faced by executives of balancing driven, focused determination with effective leadership and healthy relationships. With over twenty years of coaching clients, I can attest to this being a worthwhile outcome and have witnessed Matt's commitment to being a living embodiment of this approach. Hey, even if you have tried before, it's not too late, try again because you will definitely gain."

— **Rabbi Ezra Max** - Visionary Thinking Partner, Executive Coach, Facilitator

"If there was a lighthouse that beamed infectious optimism cutting through the grey mist to cast a web of inspiration, inside, tending to the evergreen flame of positivity, would be Matt Drinkhahn. His simple yet powerful formula of staying curious in the midst of life's challenges will surely resonate with anyone who has been caught in the oops loop—the, "damn, I did it again!" cycle that plagues us all from time to time."

— **Brent Perkins**, Author of *Papercuts: The Art of Self-Delusion*, founder of 3xBold.com and Front Row Dad

"By connecting with Matt Drinkhahn through our podcasts, I discovered the transformative power of optimism. Matt's journey, marked greatly by the loss of his father, is a testament to

turning grief and pain into driving forces for positive change. His unwavering commitment to being a better human and his knack for transforming missteps into opportunities for growth have inspired many, including myself. This book is not just a narrative; it's a beacon of hope, teaching us that every day holds the potential for improvement and positivity."

– **Matt Gilhooly**, The Life Shift Podcast

"Made any mistakes lately? Good, you're ready for a very important lesson life wants to teach you. In my experience, life keeps delivering adversity and challenge until we finally learn that lesson. My best intentions and careful planning after college ended in divorce and burnout. If not for people like Matt to help me stay positive, be curious, and show me an entirely new way of learning from my burning mess, it would never have become my breakthrough message! I'm regularly inspired by Matt's optimism and resilience, especially in the stories you'll love from this book."

— **Zach White**, CEO and Host of The Happy Engineer Podcast

"Matt is an eternal optimist, recovering perfectionist, and committed to curiosity and continuous improvement. He expertly mixes humor with sagacity and self-deprecation with deep insights derived from his personal journey of growth and discovery. Read this book, enjoy the journey, and gain fresh insights through riveting prose.

— **Brandon Miller**, Co-Author of *Play to Their Strengths* and *Incredible Parent*, CEO of 34Strong.com

"Matt Drinkhahn embodies perseverance and a positive mindset more than anyone I've ever met. He always brings a positive *can do*

perspective to any challenge that empowers him and everyone he interacts with to see possibilities where others see only roadblocks. When Matt joined me on The Mindful FIRE Podcast, I shared that because I have two young kids and I was struggling to find time for my morning routine. Matt immediately saw this struggle as an opportunity to bring my sons into my practice and deepen my bond with them. I have no doubt you'll find similar wisdom you can immediately apply to your life in the pages that follow."

— **Adam Coelho**, Dad, Husband, and Googler, Host of The Mindful FIRE Podcast

"I have known Matt Drinkhahn for quite a while; a man with greater integrity would be harder to find. He is grounded and empathetic with a really positive take on life. I love talking with him as there is always so much 'gold' in our conversations. His book *The Eternal Optimist* focuses on leadership and life. It offers the reader powerful insights into how the choices we make moment by moment impact on not only ourselves but on others too. We follow Patrick's journey as he strives to achieve the success he so badly craves but, in the process, jeopardizes the things which he values most. We discover how being well intentioned is not enough to make you a great leader. Trusting others, actively listening, and valuing the contribution of others are vital if relationships and businesses are to succeed and thrive. Matt shares these principles in an interesting and engaging way. It is a must read for anyone who desires loving interdependent personal relationships and who wants to lead their professional team as an empowering and enlightened leader."

— **Gina Gardiner**, International Book of Honour Award Winner 2023

"I've known Matt for twenty-five years and my experience with him has been one of watching a leader of leaders ascend to the top of his craft through constant optimism, great depth, and consistency. In my own experience with adversity and challenge, keeping a positive attitude has been the most important thing. I've had different times in my own business where things weren't being executed the way they should be, at times even when it caused us to operate at a loss. But having the right mental approach and staying positive through the process opened the door to success once again. I will also say that there have been times when a call to Matt helped me turn on the optimistic mindset needed to overcome that challenge. This book is like a key to being able to unlock that door because Matt is a true master at this skill."

— **Matt King**, Co-Founder with Blue Chip Maintenance

Contents

Testimonials IV

Introduction 1

Chapter 1 14

Chapter 2 25

Chapter 3 32

Chapter 4 46

Chapter 5 61

Chapter 6 75

Chapter 7 85

Chapter 8 97

Chapter 9 110

Chapter 10 122

Chapter 11 132

Chapter 12 142

Epilogue 155

About the Author. 167

More Testimonials 170

Introduction

Welcome to a book written by an eternal optimist.

It's my sincerest pleasure to bring this story to you, dear reader, as I fulfill a childhood dream of publishing a book. As I grew up, I dreamed of becoming a writer as a profession, to entertain people and make a living. Then I evolved into wanting to help people overcome their biggest fears and challenges. This paragraph illustrates how, over time, I changed my views as I gained more perspective. That's what this book is about, how we can change over time with a little curiosity, gratitude, and discipline. Buckle up for a good read, my friend!

As a "words of affirmation" guy, I'd like to share special thanks to those who have inspired me, taught me (whether they realized it or not), challenged me, and led me along the way. If this list is exhausting for you to read, feel free to jump straight to the book!

Thank you from the bottom of my heart to these very important people:

- My daughters Lily, Lucy, and Caroline. You inspire me every day (and sometimes challenge me) to be a present and loving dad. *From you I learned patience and grace.*

- My wife Julie, who has been a major influence and muse since the day we met, when I accidentally stepped on her foot. She's the yin to my yang. We're different and completely compatible. I'm hopelessly in love with her to this day. *From you I learned teamwork and seeing through the lens of others.*

- My mom Jo, the unsung hero (like most parents), who has overcome more obstacles and pains than I could or would name here. She grew up with a loving mom and siblings in the deep south, poor in money, rich with heart. She gave her all to raise me and my heart beats with eternal gratitude for her. *From you I gained gratitude, empathy, and perspective.*

- My dad Marc, God rest his soul, who I looked up to as my guide and teacher. *He taught me to value people by their character, words, and actions, not by their skin color or politics or how much money they bring in, simply by how they show up.*

On this opening page of the book, does it make sense to honor and appreciate every person who has impacted my life? It does to me, and here is an abbreviated list of those for whom I'm eternally grateful:

 My friend Phil Bohlender, with his sense of humor and unflinching faith, who has stayed strong while losing both his father and sister in the span of a month, who has recommitted to his vision and family. *From you I saw how when one is put to the emotional brink, that vision and grit can lead one through the things in life outside of their control.* Love you, my friend.

 My friend and mentor Mark Victor Hansen, who in his 70s has as much energy and vitality as a teenager and has helped me by publishing this book. *From you I've learned to ask for what I want and to play a bigger game in life.* Thank you MVH.

 My friends from the Front Row Dads. Know that this group of family men with businesses is the place to be if you align with the theme of this sentence. *Thank you, my brothers, for making it safe to open up and practice being a great dad and husband.*

My friends from XCHANGE; Jon Berghoff, Adair Cates, Steve Bouchard, Robert Murray, Natalie Alcantara, and the crew I invested two years with to help me open up my mind to the possibilities of facilitating like the BEST in the world (Jon Berghoff). This group of facilitators are overflowing with positive energy and a powerful approach to leadership called appreciative inquiry. *Thank you for empowering me with the tools to lead the world.*

 My friends and Bandmates:

- Matt Sprang, who models empathy and is constantly challenging himself and all others to grow.
- Nick Hemmert, who always makes me feel important and has the funniest self-deprecating sense of humor that always takes on the challenges in the room and relieves any self-centered ego the rest of us are feeling. He changes rooms when he speaks out. *Thank you, brother.*
- Ali Jafarian, who helped me lean towards being present and creating more space and IS the YODA of our time.
- Scott Groves, who has shown through transparent debate and authentic public accountability how one

can be in business AND share their beliefs openly and lose business while keeping their integrity.

- Ryan Levesque, who has modeled humility by sharing his challenges and his world-class business acumen through his unique and inspirational lens.

My friend Adam Stock, who helped me to transform anger into acceptance.

My friend Michael Wagner, who helped me to merge my intellect and heart into one.

My friend Tyler Gunter, who showed me courage through vulnerability and has made me better.

My friends and financial mentors:

- Justin Donald, who I knew during my Cutco years and now again in two mastermind groups. He's brilliant and focused on empowering others to build real wealth.
- Erik Van Horn, who I know as the "franchise" man who earned my respect from two actions he took.
  1. He called me a "loser" because I was simply saving money and not investing. I got in the investing game again because of that conversation.
  2. He chose family over money in a major decision. Those who know him know the story—respect.

My friend Ned Schaut, whose "Fatherhood Field Notes Podcast" and journaling techniques, coupled with his amazing commitment to being an unapologetically proud and present father, have impacted me beyond measure. He's the gold standard of Front Row Dad.

 My friend Frank Wiseman, who brought me into a business community where I've made many dear, dear friends: Brad Divins, Chris LaPata, Tony Perez, Jenna Geigerman, Savannah Enzweiler, Mendy McNeel, Alison Volckens, Sean O'Neill, Abdul Khan, Tripp Guin, LaMonte Johnson, John Christenbury, and of course John Leddy (I always bring out his best golf).

 My friends Hunter Fleshood and Jade Franklin, the power couple in Charlotte who make me laugh, challenge me to think, and always bring the energy and smiles.

 My friend Justin C. Morgan, who shared with extreme empathy and vulnerability the turbulent times of his son's cancer journey in late 2022-early 2023, I learned to be prepared and own everything about your circumstances.

 My friend Ryan Casey, who IS THE epitome of a businessman with empathy and focus on results. One can be both and he's world-class in this space.

 My friend Les McDaniel, who is an absolutely selfless giver. Thank you for asking the questions and for getting us to dig deeper as men.

 My friend Jon Vroman, who founded the Front Row Foundation and Front Row Dads, where I've literally changed the trajectory of my life forever. I love this very real, loving, intense, and vulnerable human, he's a gamechanger.

- My friend Rachael Dietrich, who invited me to meet her family in Key West at the BAGEL Store and has always greeted me with great energy.

- My brother-in-law Shaun Pasquale, whose quick wit and unflinching devotion to his friends has taught me and inspired me on how to be a great friend, not easy to do as an adult. *Thank you buddy.*

- My mother-in-law Anne Treadwell, who has taught me how to be a son-in-law, how to be patient while in love. *Love you Oma.*

- My friend Kevin Evers, who walked ninety minutes with me in San Antonio to go .4 miles, and reminds me of it every time we speak. For this fun memory, I honor him!

- My friend Matt Ticknor, who is inspiring me through his journey of personal development. He's been amazing to get to know.

- My friend Geoff Woods, who I look up to and have learned from, one of the smartest strategists and communicators I've had the privilege to call friend. He taught me how to be vulnerable publicly through his actions. He's changed my life forever.

- My friend Chris Gray, who has taught me about being a sponge and taking notes on life, all while laughing with me and helping me feel welcome in the "Cool Club" (of which he is a founding member). I salute him.

- My friend Scott Duncan from South Dakota, for teaching me about parenting teenagers and being patient with self and others, and for the classic phrase "H**** S**" (inside joke)!

- My friends Paul Gollnick and Brent Perkins, who have guided me in meditation and mindfulness. You've taught me and my family well. *I thank you dearly.*

- My friend Tucker Max, who shows up direct, real, never holding back. His direct feedback mixed with humor has kept me laughing and reflecting. *Thanks Tucker.*

- To the man who taught me to bark like a seal when things get crazy during the family rides. *Thank you Eric Farewell, I'm always listening when you speak.*

- To the men who shared their truths and inspired me through their authenticity, thank you Steve Bouchard, Doug Phillips, and Eric Post. I've invested one-on-one time with each of you and you've changed my life.

- To the greatest hockey coach/consultant on the planet, thank you PJ Atherton for showing up as the strongest man in the room, mixed with the highest caring and level of empathy, too. You're the full package, and we're lucky to be graced with your presence, brother.

- To Mike Abramowitz, who has been to the depths of heartbreak and emotional adversity. *You're an inspiration and I'll follow you where your heart leads us, my friend.*

 To the Dream Machine himself, Dane Espegard, who always has a way of making the heavy things in life seem lighter. *I love you for your sense of humor and friendship.* It helps that because of your teachings, I'm full of dreams that I've written down.

 To Steven Christopher, who very uniquely helped me to connect with my wife through humorous adult drawings that I leave hidden around the house (He's also a great friend, too!).

 To James Yaman, who encouraged me to take "Dream Walks" without conditions and has helped me to connect with my wife. *Thank you my new friend.*

 To Bret Richmond, who is always asking questions and soaking in new information. You've reminded me to be proud and confident in my inquisitive nature by modeling it yourself. *Thanks for asking the questions my friend.*

 To Kristian Nylund, who has inspired me through his true vulnerability within the first eight minutes of hearing him speak. WOW, he brought it and modeled playing all-in. *Thanks brother.*

 To Seth Dailey, who introduced me to his amazing family and welcomed me into his home, who also keeps going deep every time he speaks. *You inspire me with every detail Seth.* Go for it. I'm listening carefully every time!

To David Vanderpool, whose sly wit and deep intellect always make me want to be a better human. He's always got something serious and humorous to say that dares me to smile more, think more, laugh more, and simply give my best effort. *Thanks brother.*

To Alex Pardo, who has shared his family and energy with me in such a way that makes me want to lean more into my family and make magical memories. *Thanks brother.*

To Stathis Edel, for always calling it like it is while adding some self-deprecating commentary, and then delivering such nuggets of wisdom that Plato himself would pause to take note. *Thanks brother.*

To Stephen Rhyne, for simply being you; a gentle giant who grins and bears it when challenged. I love when you speak and I always learn. *Thanks brother.*

To Michael Scott, for having the courage to have a transparent conversation with me about what it means to be a true friend. *Thanks for pushing me.*

To Chris Coggin, whose unique perspectives on learning, money, family, curing PTSD, saving humanity, and others. *Your blend of easy-going AND intensity towards your passion inspires me brother.*

To Greg Powell, who wiped the floor with me in pickleball at the Front Row Dads retreat in Fall 2023. *I'm coming for you brother. I love a good challenge and you inspire me.*

- To my friends Savannah Royal, Tom Schneller, Charlotte King Blais who keep showing up for the daily Livestream in 2023 and honoring my by their presence and attention. *Thank you Friends!*

- My friend and client Scott Klein, who is a living legend in the financial advisory business at Equitable. He has modeled work ethic far beyond expectation and has shown he is always open to learning. He's an amazing human.

- My friend and client Sandy Solomon, one of my first podcast guests, who I coached AND he mentored me the whole time (7+ years as of the writing). *Thanks, you changed my life forever.*

- My friend and client Blair Martin, who may be the strongest leader I've ever had the privilege of coaching, for offering me a master class on setting vision and deeply caring for clients. He makes me want to be better.

- My friend and client Dillan Micus, whose story will one day be told around the world as the gold standard of how to stay F.R.E.S.H. and keep on moving forward. Mark my words, this man will impact the world in miraculous ways. Seek him out if you're reading this.

- My friends and clients Daniel Oh and Irvin Hu, who work harder and at a pace unmatched by others. They have taught me how to practice leveling up one's skills because they constantly challenge themselves to do just that.

 My friends and clients at Pace Development Group in Charlotte, NC:

- Brian Pace, the owner and relentless heart leader, who took over the company under the most painful situation and has led it to record growth during all of this—well done, impressive forever, no matter what.
- David Faulkner, for going above and beyond for all teammates and clients, (and even during someone's wedding weekend when a kid dared throw an apple at his car).
- Charlie Fonville, for modeling "no excuses, get it done, deliver to the client with the greatest attitude you can." An outstanding human.
- And the rest of this amazing Team who inspire me all the time: DeLaine, Snover, Craver, Vicki, Eric, Duane, Susan, Patti, Jenine (who loves Metallica!), and Kevin. *You ARE a high-performance team!*

 To my friend and client Mark Woodfield, whose aptitude for finance and service is unmatched, whose attitude to serve his family and clients is unparalleled. He's taught me how to manage it all while conquering perfectionism—a sincere treat to be in the Front Row watching him conduct the symphony of business.

 To my friends and clients at Rock Hill School District 3, Dr. Tommy Schmolze and Dr. John Jones. The world couldn't ask for leaders who care more and offer their people growth opportunities. *Keep leading my friends, you're guiding us all.*

 My friend Wendy Baum, one of the smartest people I've ever met, who IS the standard on following through for her clients. I learned during all four years of coaching her.

 My friend Brad Dickman, for showing up for his family in ways I cannot mention here. He has inspired me with permanent gratitude for how he IS overcoming adversity daily. You truly are the definition of "doing it for the family." *Much respect my friend.*

 My friend Dan Andrews, for showing me over a twenty-year period how to live through highs and lows and always come out on top, through attitude and persistence. I've learned so much from him.

 And last, like guest stars in movies who get the last credit, my dear friends:

- Matt King, who I've bonded with through battle, parties, deep conversation, and brotherhood. He has played a pivotal role in my external confidence by accepting me and helping me to feel like part of the "Cool Club" (he's the President). His friendship has been paramount.
- Phillip Stutts, who I've bonded with through one of the most impactful conversations of my life in 2021. I've learned how to channel my energy into what I want most while also working ON how I show up for my family. *Phillip, you are a major reason this book got written because you've modeled how to lean into personal growth.*

My friends, buckle up and let's take a dive down the rabbit hole together. This book is about your journey and making the most of it—on your terms. How might one live a life where they find meaning? How might you be able to shape your lens so that you can experience a life filled with purpose and joy? It is my strongly-held belief that anyone can do this and, through this book, I intend to show you how. Your antennae must be up and your lens must be searching for nuggets of wisdom of all sizes and shapes because they're out there. All we need to do is look. If you're not seeing them now, it's because your lens is set to an old prescription. Let's discover that new prescription together, shall we?

Chapter 1

"Would you look at that." Patrick slapped the Plexiglas partition separating him from the cabbie. "The rain stopped. This day just can't get any better." He swiped his credit card through the taxi's machine. "Hope your night's looking as good as mine."

Without waiting for a response, he stepped out of the cab at the corner of 6th and 51st and slammed the car door shut. On the sidewalk he stopped and filled his chest with a long, deep breath. This was the best day ever.

Heading up the block toward Le Bernardin, he caught his reflection in the glass-fronted buildings and was almost surprised to find his shoes were touching the sidewalk as he walked. He felt like he was floating. This was *it*. This was *the day*. He was *the man*. His brilliant idea was no longer an idea. In fact, he had a working prototype that was so successful he'd secured a second financier. They'd already sent the money his way to get the ball rolling on the project. Things were working out so beautifully that just today, he'd signed a contract with a manufacturer and landed a deal with a national retail chain—the first of many more national retail chains to come. Yes. His *brilliant* idea was coming to life. The Airwave: the world's first counter-top air-fryer/convection oven/conventional oven/microwave all in one appliance will soon be in production. This was pivotal. He was on his way to being the CEO of his own appliance company. Of course, the rain stopped. The world was his oyster. No, the world was his airwave.

Ding. He pulled his cell phone from his jacket pocket and saw a text from Erika: *Where are you? It's 9:30.*

He was a half-hour late. When did he lose that time? Whatever. She'll get over it soon enough. She had no idea he was about to make her day, too. He could picture it: a little Royal Osetra caviar and a bottle of Veuve Clicquot—no, Perrier-Jouët. That's right. Perrier--Jouët champagne was what he'd ordered to set the mood. He entered the restaurant and spotted Erika right away.

She sat at the table he'd reserved, the one positioned "just so" to give them enough privacy to talk quietly, and yet where other diners would easily be able to see their celebration. Only, she didn't look as if she was there to celebrate.

Her long blond hair, usually smooth and flowing over her shoulders was pulled up into a messy knot at the top of her head. Her beautiful face seemed puffy from across the room, and she sat slumped in her chair, as if she had no energy. While his feet still seemed to hover above the floor, her body looked crushed by the wall of ocean spray in the painting behind her.

She couldn't be *that* mad at him for being late, could she? He was always late. In fact, she was always late, too. Their Monday night dates never happened on time. He frequently

stayed late at the office, and she would often rush in from yet another rehearsal that ran overtime. Not that it mattered tonight. She'd forget how late he was soon enough.

He nodded to Charles, the maître d', and strutted over to the table. Erika watched him with emotionless eyes. She didn't smile as he approached, didn't even smirk when he stopped before her and spread his arms open wide, palms pointed up. Nor did she stand to hug or kiss him *hello*. Really? It was just a half hour.

Bending to kiss her cheek, he noticed her eyes were red and her makeup smeared.

"Everything all right?" He sat in the chair opposite her.

"Nothing is all right." She sipped white wine from an almost empty glass.

"Babe. C'mon." Patrick leaned over the table and took her hand. She let him take it and maintained a rigid fist. "Erika, sweetheart." He did that thing where he tilted his head just a little to show off the angle of his chin while he grinned. She never could resist that look. It worked, she relented, relaxed her hand, and let her fingers entwine around his.

"I'm sorry I'm late. I have the wonderful news."

"Good. I need wonderful news. It's been a horrible day. Just horrible." Erika sniffed, sat up a little straighter in her chair. "The worst one ever."

"Not possible." He squeezed her fingers. "In fact, it's the best day ever. Sure, I'm a little late to dinner, and you know it's not the end of the world. So, wipe those tears away, babe. We're going to have a great evening."

"Seriously?" She pulled her hand away. "You think I'd be this upset simply over you being late for dinner? Look at me, Patrick."

Her voice was so loud, he glanced around the room before focusing on her. He wanted to attract the other kind of attention—attention with applause. He didn't want anyone eyeing them up for making a scene. When he did finally turn his eyes to her, he realized how very sad she looked, not angry. "I'm sorry." This wasn't the way he'd planned the evening to begin. That was okay, though. He'd pivot.

He ran a hand through his short, dark hair, as he gathered his thoughts and came up with a new plan: he'd roll with it. Let her pour her heart out about whatever was going on in the theater world, and then he'd be her hero and make her so happy, nothing else about the day would matter. "I see you're upset. What's going on?"

"Let me start by telling you what's not going on." Erika's voice had a sharp tone to it that he'd only ever heard when she'd rehearse angry lines at home.

"What do you mean?"

"My . . ." her breath faltered. "My show is not going on."

"Of course not." He gave a dismissive wave with his hand. "It's Monday. No real shows are going on—"

"Ever." Erika pressed the heels of her hands against her eyes. "It's not *ever* going on," she wailed.

She was being a bit dramatic in Patrick's view, a habit he'd often forgiven her for. In fact, he'd joked with the guys

at the golf course that it was an occupational hazard for actresses—on occasion, they carried the drama off stage. He always saw it as a fun challenge to turn her emotions around and make her smile. In a way, her apparent despair right now was perfect for him. It made the challenge of turning her evening around a little more difficult, which meant the payoff would be even more amazing. He was ready for this game. Just needed a few more clues as to what was going through her mind.

"Um, so you mean . . ." He had to force himself not to grin.

"I mean . . ." she raked her hands over her head and pulled out the band holding the knot of hair back. "The financial backers pulled out of the production. The show is canceled."

She looked so cute. Her tousled hair fell over her shoulders in a most endearing way. She tilted her head down so her blue eyes looked up at him from under her brows. She even pouted a little. Aha. That was her game. Cute.

"Good thing you got me, babe." He leaned back in his chair and full-on smiled. Once more, he held his arms out wide, palms pointed up. "I'll take care of you."

"What?"

"Trust me. You may not realize it yet, though I promise you, today is the greatest day of your life." He glanced around to find Charles so he could give him the signal. Eye contact accompanied by two quick nods and then Charles would tell the waiter to begin *the plan* by bringing out the champagne. "In fact—"

"How can you be so insensitive?" Erika's words were much too loud. She nearly shrieked. Everyone in the restaurant probably heard her.

"Shh. Babe." He touched a forefinger to his lips as he leaned over the table toward her. "I get it. I know this was an important part for you—"

"This was not just a part, Patrick." She said the words in a staccato rhythm, hitting the Ts and K hard. "This was my first lead role."

"I know. And you got that lead because you're good at what you do, great even. That means this was the first of many more coming to you. I just know it. Now's not the time for tears, babe." He tried to reach for her again. She leaned even further away, hands crossed over her heart.

"It's taken me ten years." Tears dribbled from her denim blue eyes, down her cheeks. "Ten years of working my way up from playing a tree in the background of a children's production of *Oz* to being in the ensemble cast of half the off-Broadway shows produced, to finally getting bit parts in the bigger shows, to side characters to . . . to *this*. This was my *dream*, and it was just taken away from me."

Now the drama was a little over the top, even for her. It was getting ridiculous. He needed to nip it in the bud before it ruined his night. He caught Charles' eye and gave the double nod. "Erica, I'm sorry if I seem insensitive. I just don't get why this one setback is such a dream crusher. It's not like all of Broadway had the plug pulled so none of the lights work anymore. There will be other

gigs, you'll get that starring role one day."

Erica reached around to her purse where it hung on the back of her chair. While she rummaged through it, Patrick felt in his pocket for the box and pulled it out, while he kept it resting on his leg, hidden under the table.

The waiter approached the table. "Is it time, sir?" He'd asked the question perfectly. Maybe the night would now turn around and go the way Patrick had organized.

Patrick winked. "We're ready now."

The waiter flicked his gaze across the table to Erika then back again and raised his eyebrows as if in question.

"Trust me," Patrick said to the man. "Everything will work out just fine."

"Patrick." Erika snapped as the waiter retreated.

"Yes?" It took him a minute to meet Erika's eyes drilling into him, as he was focused on noting where the waiter went. He'd need to watch for the man to re-appear with the champagne so he could time things just right.

"I'm not in the mood to be here right now." Erika wiped her nose with a tissue and shook her hair away from her face. "I think I need to go home."

"You can't." He gripped tighter to the box on this lap. "You have to stay here for dinner."

"You don't get to tell me what to do." She threw the wrinkled tissue back in her purse. "And you don't seem to care about my feelings—"

"That's not true. I've done nothing except care about your feelings all night-all day."

Erika pushed her chair back from the table, as if she

were really leaving and froze in place. "Good thing you never wanted to be an actor, Patrick. Because you're really crappy at it." He spotted what looked like a snarl on her face. What was the matter with her?

"Wait. Please." With the box clamped tight in one hand, he quickly stretched across the table to grab hold of hers again with the other. "This dinner was meant to be special. It's our favorite restaurant."

"Your."

"What?"

"It's *your* favorite restaurant. Mine is the Skylark."

Patrick blinked at her. That didn't seem right to him. She'd never mentioned that, had she? Maybe. He seemed to recall her mentioning it a few, or maybe several times. "Well, we're here now. The food is excellent, and really Erika, I do have good news."

Patrick felt the tension leave her body a little. He released her hand, took a deep breath, and leaned back while she scooted her chair closer to the table. His smile took over his face as soon as he thought about the deal he'd just landed. "My Airwave—"

"That again?" She rehung her purse on the chairback and folded her arms across her chest.

"Yes, ha," he laughed. "*That* again. I know it probably seems like that's all I've been talking about lately—"

"Not 'seems.' It *has* been all you've talked about lately."

"Well, babe, all that talk is paying off. Today, I signed a contract with a manufacturer and landed a national account. Airwaves will be sold all across this country soon."

"Good for you." Her face softened as she nodded. "Seriously, Patrick. I'm happy your dream is coming true."

Perfect timing, he could see the waiter on the way over. "Well, only part of it is coming true. The other part will come true if you say 'yes' to this question." He left his chair, knelt on one knee, and opened the ring box. "Erika, will you marry me?"

She was speechless. He watched her face, waiting for the confusion to be replaced by joy.

"I, um—" was all that came out of her. She still looked confused.

He took the ring out of the box, placed it on her finger, and stood up.

"Patrick." She gazed at the ring, twisted it side to side. The light refracted through the diamonds in a dazzling way. "It's . . . it's so beautiful."

"And the contract is so big, that you can quit this Broadway thing. I'll take care of you. You won't need to work."

"What?"

"You can stay home all day—"

"How dare you talk to me that way?" Erika stood. "Who are you? Are you even human?"

"Shh, sweetheart." Patrick placed his hands on her arms. Once more he looked around. Yes, people were staring at them. This wasn't going as planned. "Don't you get it? It doesn't matter that you lost the show. You still got me."

She wiggled away from him. "And maybe that's not

what I want." Before he could respond, she ripped the ring off her finger and threw it at him. She slung her purse over her shoulder and stormed past.

He turned and watched her go, realizing the waiter had stopped in his tracks. He held a bottle of champagne in one hand, an ice bucked in another, and a little folding table was hung on one arm. His face was impassive; his eyes, however, clearly told Patrick he wasn't sure what to do.

A shocked couple stared from a nearby table. Patrick shrugged at them. "What can you do?" He bent over and picked up the ring. No one dared to answer him.

Whatever. It was still a great day. He had signed the manufacturing contract. He had landed the national deal. "There's still plenty to celebrate." He waved the waiter toward him. "Let's open that champagne."

"Are you sure, sir?" the waiter set the ice bucket on the foldout table.

"Absolutely. She'll be fine when she settles down. I've got it all under control."

Erika will regret she missed out on the caviar, too. He was sure of it.

Chapter 2

W hat was that sound? Oh, his phone was ringing. Where was it? Not on the nightstand.

Sunlight streamed in through the slit in the bedroom curtains. Patrick realized he was still in his slacks and shirt from the night before. Right. He'd wound up downing the whole bottle of champagne before coming home and crashing in his clothes. Thankfully, he'd taken off his shoes and tie. What time was it?

The phone silenced. He fumbled around in the sheets on his bed looking for it. Erika wasn't beside him. Scenes from last night fluttered through his head. Buzzed from the alcohol, he had come home to a dark apartment. A dark and empty apartment. Erika wasn't anywhere to be found.

Maybe she was who called? He found his cell in his slacks pocket—he'd slept with his phone in his pocket. It wasn't Erica who'd called, it was Thad, his brand-new CFO.

He should call her. And he would as soon as he spoke to Thad. Why would he be calling so early in the morning? He returned the call.

"My man, Thad. Good morning." It was easy for Patrick's voice to be enthusiastic. He loved having a CFO:

it was another sign of being successful. He had resigned from his sales job at Samsung as soon as he'd received confirmation from the first financial backer. As the dream slowly became reality, he checked off one item after another: a full C-suite, his own corner office, an assistant . . .

"Where are you?" Thad wanted to know.

"Home." Patrick pulled the cell away from his face far enough to see the time. Yikes. It was seven o'clock. He should be at work by now. "I'll be in the office in half an hour."

"Actually, you got forty-five minutes. Only don't come to the office."

"I don't understand." He sat up in the bed. He hadn't drunk *that* much last night. Why didn't he know what was going on?

"The name Jax Aaronson ring any bells?"

"Loud and clear." Jax was the head buyer for Home Life, the largest home goods retailer in the nation, soon to be world if what the *Wall Street Journal* was reporting was true.

"He's staying at the TWA Hotel out near JFK Airport. He's about to leave the country for an extended trip in Europe and is interested in meeting you over coffee at seven-forty-five. He wants to hear all about the Airwave. This might be your one and only chance to get us into Home Life."

"I'll be there." Patrick clicked out of the call and jumped out of bed. Erika's note crunched under his socked foot.

He picked it up, sat on the edge of the bed, and tried to flatten it out to read it again. When he'd first found it last night, placed on his pillow like a scene prop in a show, he'd

rolled his eyes. How long was she going to play this game, he wondered. Wasn't it enough all ready? He'd crumpled it up and threw it on the floor before falling into bed and conking out.

Reading it now, in a streak of sunlight crossing through their otherwise dim bedroom, it felt less like a game, and more like a boxing match. One where he'd been punched in the gut. She was gone. Her curly handwriting didn't tell him where or when she'd come back. Though it did tell him why she left: *You lied to me. You don't love me. You only love yourself. I'm through.*

How could she think that way? They'd been together for years. He'd supported her as she moved up through the ranks on Broadway, had sent her enormous bouquets at the end of every performance, had . . .

He shook his head. He'd deal with that later. Right now, he needed to get ready to make the biggest deal of his life. Sure, he could send in Nico, his newly hired head of sales, however, in this case, this fish was too big to trust anyone else. He, himself, had to reel it in.

He plugged his phone in to charge on his nightstand and glanced at the empty space where Erika should be sleeping. Where was she? How could she just up and leave on the night he proposed to her? They'd been together for five years. They were committed to each other. How often had they spoken about getting married one day when things were right? Weren't they right, now? Didn't he just tell her things were right last night? He'd just landed the first national deal.

He re-read the note. It almost sounded like she was gone for good. Actually, not almost, it did sound as if she was gone for good. What was she thinking? They had both signed the lease on their Upper West-side walk-up apartment. Granted, she couldn't afford half the monthly rent, so they prorated things. He never minded. He understood it was hard work to make a decent living on Broadway. Why couldn't she understand she no longer needed to do that? She could get a different job now, maybe outside the theater where they'd actually have time to be together instead of only Monday nights. Why couldn't she realize he was setting them up for the perfect life?

A heaviness filled his chest. A lump formed in his throat.

Enough. He wadded up the note from Erika once again. This time he threw it away in the wastebasket beside the bed. Thinking about her and asking questions only she could answer wasn't doing him any good. He had the biggest sales call of his life to make. He needed to get ready.

He prepped his coffee machine to make a cup then hit the shower, where he rehearsed the lines he'd say to Jax Aaronson as he washed. He recently read an article on the man in *Forbes*. He'd review that while in the cab. Jax had spoken about scaling teams, the challenges that crop up when finding the right balance of managing and empowering your people. Yeah, he'd bring that up, they'd bond over that. Jax had been instrumental in Home Life's stratospheric business growth. That's what he wanted for his company: stratospheric business growth. Maybe Patrick could learn from him. How proud his parents would be. His dad wasn't

thrilled with him leaving Samsung to start his own company. Just wait until Dad sees what becomes of Patrick.

Yes. He was making it happen. He was fulfilling his dream. He was—alone. He'd ripped open the closet door and discovered it was half empty. Three-quarters empty was more like it. Everything Erika had in there was gone.

When did she do that? Probably when he was sucking down that caviar and champagne. Then he'd eaten the full chef's tasting menu. That lobster was magnificent. How could Erika not love that restaurant? Not that it mattered right now. All her clothes, even every single pair of shoes the woman owned, were gone.

Still wrapped in a towel, he investigated the bedroom. All her drawers were empty. The only thing on her nightstand were the lamp, a book on leadership he'd found inspirational and wanted her to read, and a storage container from the kitchen filled with jewelry. Picking up an earring, he realized it was all the jewelry he'd ever given her.

Yeah, she meant she was gone for good. Pressure built behind his eyes. He closed the lids, sniffed, and struggled to get his breath back to normal. No. This was a minor blip. She was throwing a really big fit and when they made up, it would be one for the books. And they *would* make up. Because . . . what else could they do? He should call her now. Maybe her head would be clearer. Maybe she'd listen to him. Surely, she'd understand now. He had their lives planned out. And the business was coming along so well.

That's what he needed to get back to. Yes, he'd reel in this big fish, get the business running and expanding

on a solid foundation and then he'd figure out the Erika mess. Right now though, he needed to continue to secure his business.

Jax Aaronson. Yes. The Airwave was about to take over the world, one kitchen at a time.

Chapter 3

Patrick slammed the door of his Porsche 911 then wiped his fingerprints off his baby with his sleeve. The car looked good in his parents' Connecticut driveway. If only the fall leaves would have lasted through to Thanksgiving. *That* would have made the picture even more perfect.

"There he is." Mom's voice sailed down the sidewalk as he rounded the front of his car. She held the storm door open, standing tall with her auburn hair pulled back in a ponytail. Even if it weren't Thanksgiving, he'd know by the ponytail that she'd spent the day in the kitchen; it was her trademark look when she cooked.

Patrick retrieved his overnight bag from the passenger seat, shut that door, and wiped his fingers from it as he had the driver's. "What do you think, Mom?" He waved to the car behind him as he headed up the walk toward her. "Isn't she gorgeous?"

"Just lovely." Mom's blue eyes flashed as she laughed. "I see you're still a car guy. After all this time in the city, I figured you'd have given up on cars by now. Don't tell me you sit in Manhattan traffic in that thing."

"Of course not." Patrick kissed her cheek. "I didn't

exactly buy it because I needed transportation, you know."

Mom held the door for him as he entered his childhood home. "I guess Erika couldn't get away for the weekend?"

"Oh, she, um, we're not together anymore." He stopped in the foyer, near the bottom of the stairs. "Didn't I tell you?"

"No. Though I had a feeling. I rather noticed she'd been absent in your talk during our phone calls—our rare phone calls."

"Mom, I've been so busy with work."

"I'm sure. Still, I miss hearing your voice, you know." She closed the door and turned toward him, her hand over her heart. "Seriously, are you all right?"

"Why wouldn't I be?"

"Erika. The breakup. When did it happen?"

Patrick waved a dismissive hand. "Jeesh, like eight months ago, I guess. You know, it wasn't any big deal, really. I just realized that she and I were not in sync. We didn't have the same life goals."

"I'm sorry, Patrick." Mom approached him with an outstretched hand. "You two had been together for a long time. That must have been hard on you. How are you handling it?"

"I'm fine." He took her hand and tugged her into a bear hug. "Honestly. Never been better. The business is skyrocketing. I've been so busy with it, I haven't thought of Erika at all. And honestly, I know I'm better off as a single man right now. I'm not ready for marriage. Just too busy with the company."

"Well, I'm glad you weren't too busy for Thanksgiving dinner with us."

"Never. Now, let me get settled in up in my old room, and I'll be down in a sec to tell you and Dad all about it."

Upstairs, he found his old boyhood bedroom had been updated, yet someone, probably Mom, had kept quite a few of his childhood treasures. On an etagere set between two windows were trophies from the golf team he captained in high school, a framed certificate from the debate team championships, and other signs of youthful achievements. It was a little strange how now, while actively in the process of his biggest achievement ever, he still had that nagging question inside him: was this good enough? Did he measure up to everyone's expectations of him? Much of what he tried to do was live up to the legacy of his family name, to carry on the torch, to continue the progression. The expectations were daunting. In order to exceed them, he had to embody *more*. By doing more, working more, focusing more, trying harder . . . he could have anything he wanted. But what did he really want? He'd know it when he found it. In the meantime, go all-in with relentless determination and integrity. This meant sacrifice, commitment, consistent practice, and self-reflection. No one could apply more pressure than Patrick. Seemed he had much more to do.

He picked up a photograph from his college graduation. There he was, standing between his parents in his purple NYU robe. Dad had gone to Columbia, where he now teaches as an adjunct professor on a part-time basis. Why hadn't Patrick been able to get into Columbia? NYU was

great, even if it wasn't Ivy League. Dad probably would have preferred he'd gone to his alma mater or another Ivy. And look at Dad now; just sold his financial planning company. He and Mom could live like royalty. Everything was perfect for them. The way he was trying to make it perfect for himself and . . . well, for just himself right now. He hadn't stopped working long enough to think about Erika much. He'd told Mom the truth: she wasn't in sync with him. It took her leaving for him to realize it. Actually, when he thought about it, he was glad she did break it off. He'd been too busy to notice that they weren't right for each other.

He was sure the right life partner would come along sooner or later. She'd be like Mom, someone with a sensible job, not a Broadway actress. As a high-school English teacher Mom had been off work during all his summer and school breaks, and her schedule fit right in with Dad's. Yes, that's the kind of life he wanted. Surely, that's what they were expecting of him, too. Erika's profession didn't fit in with that at all.

Movement outside the window caught his eye. He approached it and watched a sleek black Mercedes travel up the driveway. Pressing his face against the glass, he was able to see Uncle David and Aunt Becky get out of the car. Not a surprise, they came every year for Thanksgiving. Wait until they hear about his company's success.

#

"Nancy." Aunt Becky stood behind a dining room

chair and fingered her pearl necklace. "You just outdo yourself every year. This dinner looks amazing."

"Thank you, Becky. You know I'll do anything to keep this tiny family together." Mom hugged her sister. "Now please, everyone sit and eat. There's too much food and so few of us. I'm afraid I might be making gluttons of us tonight."

Patrick smiled at his little family and predicted how the evening would go down. The conversation was the same every year. Aunt Becky, who was renowned for being a terrible cook, would lavish praise on Mom's finesse in the kitchen. Uncle David and Dad would find excuses to leave the room to check out the scores of the football games. It would be another delicious meal, only this time the conversation wouldn't be boring—it wouldn't be about his married cousins who all lived far away and would be coming in to visit Uncle David and Aunt Becky for Christmas; it wouldn't be about Mom and Dad's latest exotic travel plans or house renovation ideas. This time he wouldn't feel like the spare tire hidden in the trunk.

"Well, Mom, I have a gift for you." Patrick made a dent in his mashed potatoes to pool the gravy.

"A gift?" Mom passed a serving dish laden with asparagus to Uncle David who, as Patrick predicted, took exactly two stalks because he much preferred dessert over asparagus.

"Yes. I guess you could say Christmas is coming early for you this year."

"How exciting. What is it?"

"It's an Airwave." He ladled on the gravy. "Though I guess I should have come early so you could use it for today."

"What's an Airwave?" Of course, Aunt Becky would ask that. According to Uncle David, she hadn't even mastered the microwave to melt butter.

"It's only the fastest-growing kitchen appliance on the market." Excitement bubbled up in Patrick. He watched his father's face, waiting for the approving look. "It's—"

"Oh, I've seen commercials for that thing." Uncle David tipped his wine glass toward him. "If anyone in my house ever thought about cooking, I'd get one. They sound like miracle workers."

"I do think about cooking." Aunt Becky cut into her turkey. "I just don't go beyond thinking."

"Which is probably a very good thing." Uncle David laughed.

"Right, well," Patrick needed to regain their attention. "I, um, you do realize that's my company, right?"

There was a pause in the clinking of forks on plates.

"You don't say?" Aunt Becky seemed to look sideways at Uncle David before smiling at Patrick. "*Your* company? Are you selling for them now?"

"Is this air . . ." Dad waved an arm back and forth. "This air thing, is it why you left that secure job at Samsung?"

Would he ever be proud of him? And 'air thing'? Didn't he realize how big this was? "Well, yes, Dad. Once I secured funding for the manufacturing, I really didn't have time to work at Samsung *and* at my own company."

"What is the product, exactly?" Dad's furrowed brows made Patrick feel smaller in his seat.

"It's an appliance, um, a kitchen appliance." Patrick forced himself to sit straight and tall. He'd won an award from *Better Homes and Gardens*. Why can't he get those words out of his mouth?

"It's another kitchen gadget?" Aunt Becky sipped her wine.

"Tell me about it, son." Mom gazed lovingly at him, or was it condescending? Was she looking down on him? No. She was always on his side.

"Well, it's the first ever countertop combination microwave, air-fryer, and conventional oven." He cleared his throat. Mom's turkey, which was usually delicious, felt like cardboard in his mouth. "Up until now, people had to have three separate appliances to do the job of this one. And it sits right on the countertop, the size of a toaster oven. It was all my idea."

"Why didn't you sell the idea to Samsung?" Dad still didn't look pleased as he cut into his turkey.

"Samsung has their tried-and-true kitchen package: fridge, range, microwave, and dishwasher. This is too revolutionary."

"Hmm." Dad chewed and frowned. "And no one wanted it?"

"Dad, I didn't want to sell it to anyone. I have always known, in my heart, that I wanted to be an entrepreneur. This was my opportunity to make my dream come true. I thought of this product. I got the patent for it. I had a

prototype made, and then I secured the funding necessary to meet orders coming in from retailers; of which there are plenty." Patrick could feel heat rising in his face. He knew the words came out sounded harsher than how he should speak at a family dinner. He cleared his throat and tried to reign in his anger and disappointment.

"I'm all for supporting a dream opportunity," Dad pointed his fork at him, "as long as it's stable."

"Gregory," Mom cast her eyes toward Dad, "why don't you and Patrick take time after dinner to discuss it privately."

Great. Mom didn't believe in this, either. Was she expecting Dad to talk Patrick out of following through on this? Didn't she see his Porsche 911? He was succeeding!

"This is why you make such a big meal, isn't it?" Uncle David held a shopping bag full of leftovers aloft. "I get to eat home-cooked meals for a full week?"

"I will always take care of my favorite brother-in-law." Mom gave him a hug. "Oh, I almost forgot. I have a bag of desserts in the kitchen."

"How could anybody forget dessert?" Uncle David helped Aunt Becky into her coat.

"You *should* forget dessert more often," she chided. "Patrick, can you invent a gadget that will zap desserts to make them as healthy as vegetables next year? Your uncle is in need."

"Ha," Patrick's laugh was forced, sounded hollow

to him as he opened the door for his aunt and uncle. His Airwave was a joke to them. They weren't his target customer; therefore, it shouldn't have bothered him. Still, why weren't they the least bit proud?

He shut the door after them and turned to go upstairs.

"Patrick?" His father's voice came from the other side of the living room. "Why don't you join me in here for a few minutes. There are probably two glasses left of that Cabernet—it's too good to go to waste."

Dad already had the wine poured by the time Patrick made it to the library. It was very sensuous in there: rich, leather armchairs the color of cognac, deep green on the walls, rows and rows of books on walnut shelves. Everything in the room was perfect from the first edition classics in the bookcase to the crystal decanters on the intricate dry bar Mom found on a shopping trip to India, to the exceptional Cabernet Dad had poured him. Yes, this is the life he was building toward. Such comfort. Such elegance. Granted, such a price tag.

"Well, Patrick, tell me about this . . . this air business you have." He sat in one of the armchairs by the fireplace and waved to the chair opposite him.

Patrick took it, feeling nervous, jittery, as if he were on a job interview. "Well, it's called an Airwave."

"Where'd you get that name from?"

"Combination of air fryer and microwave. It . . ."

"Didn't you say it was a mix of three things?"

"Yes, everyone knows an air fryer is kind of like an oven. Besides, we'd have to call it an air-o-wave or whatever. It wouldn't sound right. And . . ."

"Where do you have it manufactured?"

"Right now, in China. I just . . ."

"Why didn't you try to sell it to a company like Whirlpool? Or Viking? One that would make it in this country?"

"Why do you have to question everything I do?" Patrick gripped tight to the wine glass. "Honestly, Dad. What's so hard about saying, 'good job, son?'"

"Good job, son. What is wrong Patrick? I just want to know more about this company."

"Why? So you can find more fault with it?" Patrick stood and downed his wine.

"I don't understand the need for the attitude, Patrick." Dad, as always, was the poster child of calm. Always confident and self-assured. It all felt like another slap in the face to Patrick. He could never live up to being like his dad.

"My company, the Airwave, are big deals, Dad. Households across the country are buying them up."

"That's great."

"Do you mean that?" Patrick couldn't tell if his father was just placating him now. "Because honestly, it is great. My company is poised to become the next major mover in the kitchenwares industry."

"What's the forward plan?" Dad sipped his Cabernet.

"What do you mean?" Patrick returned to his seat.

"You can't rest your laurels on one product." Dad extended his index finger from his wine glass and pointed it toward Patrick. "If this really is so good that you could safely leave Samsung and are . . . what did you say?"

"What?" Patrick was stuck on the fact that Dad couldn't let Samsung go.

"Poised to take over the kitchenwares industry. I believe you said that. Well, if you really are poised, what's next? What's the next product?"

"I don't know yet. We haven't even been rolled out for a year—"

"Then you're not really poised for anything are you?"

Patrick flew out of his chair again. "Are you serious? Even Uncle David has heard of my product. Everyone knows about it. My business is expanding like nothing anyone has seen. If you were still in financial planning, you'd be telling everyone to keep their eye on me."

He stormed out of the library. He should just go home now. No. He'd had a couple glasses of wine. Better to just sleep it off and get out of here first thing in the morning. Leave this place before his judgmental father was even out of bed.

He tossed and turned all night, rehashing the conversation with his Dad. Why was it so hard for the man to be proud of him?

His mother was in the kitchen when he entered it the next morning.

"What are you doing up this early?" She stirred fresh blueberries into a mixing bowl. Must be making a blueberry buckle, one of Patrick's favorite treats.

"I'm heading back to the office." He had to get back to where he belonged; back to where he was understood and appreciated.

"Not this early. I thought we'd have you for the whole weekend."

"I'm sorry, Mom." He kissed her cheek. "I have an empire to run."

Maybe not an empire just yet, and one day, his father would look at what he did and finally appreciate his son and his genius move to leave his stable job at Samsung.

Outside, he threw his bag onto the passenger seat, paused to wipe his prints off the passenger door, and then climbed behind the driver's seat. The growl of the engine thrilled him. Maybe he should stay long enough to be sure his dad saw the car. Nah. He'd just have to see it another time.

It was hard to keep his foot light on the gas pedal going down the driveway. His baby was meant for speed. He let her open up more and more the further he made it away from his childhood home. As the speed increased, his mood improved.

This was the first Christmas shopping season with the Airwave in existence. Everyone would need one for their holiday dinners. He was making home cooking easier, faster, and more convenient for thousands of people— eventually millions.

Out on the Merritt Parkway, he pretty much had the road to himself. He let his Porsche 911 Turbo engine do what she does best and reward him with tight handling and fast speeds. Yes. He was the man. He knew he was a success, his product was the *it* product of the season. Everything was lining up perfectly.

Uh oh. Red and blue flashing lights came up behind him. He slowed. The lights grew closer. *Darn it.* He had been obsessing again about the future he was creating, and he'd lost track of his speed. This was an unnecessary mistake. He didn't make them often and when he did, he was extra critical of himself. One noteworthy advantage he'd cultivated over time was how he spoke to himself in times like these when mistakes were made. Once upon a time it was *I can't believe I did that,* followed by built-up suppressed emotion that stuck with him. Today it was an instant of frustration where his inner voice told him, *Shake it off. You can do better than this.* And poof. Like a rainstorm that suddenly broke, the emotion was gone, frustration over, and he was back. He owed a debt of gratitude to his father for teaching him this, although his father hadn't mastered it yet. It's okay though. Once he built his empire and gained his dad's approval, he'd teach his dad this skill. Life is a long journey. He'd have the time later to do that.

Back to the moment.

Despite him praying the police officer would go around him, he was pulled over anyway.

When you have a Porsche like his, you don't get little tickets. *Wow,* he thought. *That was a ticket. Oh well, I deserved it. The officer was just doing his job.* It was a solemn reminder to stay focused on what he was supposed to be doing. Get to the office. Get to work. He was right where he was supposed to be.

Chapter 4

Patrick slowed as he approached the turn for his apartment. He really didn't want to go home. He had a whole day ahead of him with nothing to do at home. Never one for hitting the malls on black Friday, he usually spent the day lounging at his parent's home, eating leftovers, checking in with old friends from high school and college on social media. The thought of hanging in his apartment all day scrolling through feeds filled with holiday meals and happy family gatherings had little appeal.

Instead of turning on his blinker, he sped up and past his street. He'd go to the office. No one else would be there. He could be productive in the quiet still of the place. He'd create a plan to double business within the next year. Maybe then, at the next Thanksgiving meal, his father would be able to say, "Good job, son. I'm proud of you."

The cafeteria on the ground floor of the high rise where his corporate office was located had little to eat that morning.

"Sorry, sir." The cashier looked bored. "We didn't expect many people would be in to work today."

"I understand. No big deal," he said, always wanting to show empathy for the people who worked in the building. He cheered her with his coffee cup. "A bagel and cream

cheese will hold me." He should have thought to ask Mom for leftovers. "Make it a great day, my friend." It was his customary goodbye to most people, his attempt at spreading some positivity to others.

He had the elevator to himself. Wasn't sure that had ever happened before. How could this many people be taking the day off from work? Maybe he should have named his company Ants, Inc. after the old fable about the ants who worked hard all year and the lazy grasshopper who would have starved if it weren't for the kindness of the ants. *Pause, hold on*, he thought. *Try to be patient with others.* The reason he's here is because he made a break from the pack. This badge of work ethic was a variable he could control, and it was an important one that was branded into his DNA. The patience and empathy came from mom and the relentless drive from dad. He was so grateful for both of them. This would be his way of paying homage to mom; a product that could serve everyone and impact the world. And it all began right now as the elevator door opened.

His ritual of full immersion into his work at the faintest signs of slowdown or opportunity over weekends and evenings, and over family holiday weekends . . .

This was the Breakfast of Champions. Could he be the first businessman on the cover of Wheaties? Ha!

He paused before the door of his suite of offices, relishing in how good it felt to know he created Strong Appliances. It could have been his full last name, Armstrong. However, this wasn't a family thing. This was Patrick's company. He was the man. He led Strong.

Pumped and excited to continue building his empire, he headed straight to his office. Seated in a forest green leather chair behind his authentic mid-century desk, he laughed as he rolled up his shirt sleeves. He was ready to put in the work to double his revenue over the next year—beginning now—today.

He powered up his computer and opened the portal to gain access to the contact details of his current and prospective clients. He'd work from A to Z in both lists. Find out what each group wanted, expected, and how they could be incentivized to buy more. Then he'd strategize on how to fulfill those wants, expectations, and incentives.

Voice mail after voice mail told him not to expect any answers until Monday. Monday? It was ridiculous that so many people were off work. Was shopping really that important? Granted, if they were all buying the Airwave, he had to admit, then yeah . . . shopping was that important. Still, somebody had to be paying for all those purchases and keeping the world running. There had to be more like Patrick out there.

Finally, in the middle of the customers whose last names began with G, Patrick got a real, live person on the other end of the phone.

"Hello?" Bill Grist answered. Odd, that wasn't very professional.

"Hey, Bill. It's Patrick from Strong."

"Who?"

Did he misdial? "Patrick Armstrong, CEO of Strong Appliances. Have I reached Bill Grist?"

"I'm sorry? Yes, you did. This is my personal cell phone. Your name didn't come up on caller ID. Can I help you?"

Patrick scribbled a note to find the personal cell numbers of more of his current customers. That was it. If they were all off work, they wouldn't be answering their work phones. "Well, I'm calling to see how I can help you and your company. I'm sure, like me, you're expecting to expand your reach into the market, and—"

"Wait. You're calling me on Thanksgiving weekend to discuss business?"

"Did I catch you at a bad time?"

"My youngest son's home from college, my oldest daughter flew in from California with her fiancé who we met for the first time yesterday."

"Oh, well, I only need a few minutes of your time."

"You can have them . . . next week." *Click.*

Well, that was unnecessary. Did he really need to be so rude? Patrick wanted to make the man rich. Two minutes of his time wasn't worth *that*?

Maybe Patrick needed to partner with better companies. With companies who *wanted* growth, who *wanted* business. He plugged on with the list until his grumbling stomach told him he needed another bagel. The café was closed. How was that possible? It was just one-thirty in the afternoon, on a Friday—in Manhattan. Everyone should be expected to be working right now. This was absolutely ridiculous.

Back up in his suite of offices, he raided the vending machines in the breakroom. It wouldn't be the most nutritious lunch ever, thankfully the carbs would give him

a little energy. As would the coffee. He made a fresh pot and headed back to the office.

Maybe the caffeine will help him get his mojo going a little. He'd made it through his current clients by this point, only getting a couple of them on the phone. None seemed to be happy to be taking a work call, however, he did get the answers that would help him strategize to meet expectations going forward. Thus far, none of the prospects seemed to be open. Maybe they weren't the right kind of company to be working with. Maybe he needed to get his sales force to find better leads—ones who valued working for a living.

It was just strange for him. There he was, the head of a company making one of the must-have appliances on the market totally unable to connect with the retail buyers and decision makers on the busiest shopping day of the year. None of those people were actually working on the sales floor. Surely, they'd want to be making deals to keep their doors open and the customers flying in all the time.

Finally, Amanda Hollingsworth answered her work phone. Yes!

"Hello, Amanda. This is Patrick from Strong Appliances."

"Patrick? Strong? From the States? Are you in London?" Amanda's British accent sounded surprised the way it lilted up a note at the end of her questions.

"No, I'm calling from my office in New York. How are you?"

"I'm well, thank you. Actually, to be honest, I'm a bit

knackered. It's almost nineteen hundred hours here. Oh, you Yanks would say seven o'clock in the evening. I've been at it since dawn. Just about to close up shop for the weekend."

"Then I caught you just in time." Finally, someone who understood the importance of hard work and putting in the time.

"I suppose so. How can I help you?"

"Well," Patrick clicked through to the notes on her file. She was the buyer for a small appliance outlet in the United Kingdom. She'd met him and Nico at a trade show in Montreal. "I'm just following up with you once more after the trade show last month. What do you think of the Airwave?"

"Oh, um. Well, I spoke with Nico just last week."

Patrick continued scrolling through the notes. There was nothing about that. He'd need to have a word with Nico. Patrick needed to know everything going on in this company. "Right, well, to follow up on what you spoke about, how are you feeling about things?"

"As I said, I think there would be modest interest here, most likely among the better healed who have larger kitchens."

"Better healed? We are striving to keep the costs under control so that everyone can buy one."

"That's lovely, really. However, if you want the British masses to purchase it, you'll need to redesign it for a smaller footprint. A much smaller footprint. British kitchens are not as large as American ones in general. And we simply don't have as much counter space."

"Interesting." This was the kind of feedback he needed. *Why hadn't Nico found this out?*

"Otherwise, I think it's a brilliant idea."

"Amanda, I cannot thank you enough for your feedback. This has been incredibly helpful."

"Very good. I really must go now. I'm about to nod off. Besides, isn't this a holiday for you?"

"Yesterday was."

"Right, well, we even have Black Friday sales here. Shouldn't you be out shopping for your friends and family?"

"I took care of that already. No rest for the weary here." Ideas for a smaller version of the Airwave filled Patrick's head. There could be plenty of uses for them here in America.

He hung up and decided to hold off calling any more prospects. Amanda Hollingsworth just gave him the best idea ever.

Within minutes, Patrick set up camp in the conference room. He wanted the big table because he liked to hash out ideas on paper and spread them out to see everything at once. Armed with a fresh cup of coffee and another load up of vending machine junk food, he scribbled and sketched with the hum of the overhead lights keeping him company.

Dorms—why hadn't he thought of that before? Dorms would be the perfect place for a much smaller version of the Airwave. He drew up mock dorm rooms with the newly designed Airwave stationed over a tiny fridge. Maybe, just maybe, Strong Appliances could re-invent the refrigerator,

too. They could be paired with the Airwaves. Both could be shrunken into smaller formats so they can fit into dorms together.

Hotels—yes, he could partner with large hotel chains. The larger Airwave units would be for the luxury suites, the smaller ones for the economy rooms.

Of course, companies like his could use them in their breakrooms. In fact, if he'd had one in his breakroom, he'd be able to eat a real meal today.

Actually, no, he wouldn't.

His mind seemed to shut off new thoughts for a brief moment. All he could think about was Mom making that blueberry buckle this morning. *Wow, that was just*

this morning. He looked at the papers scattered over the conference table. He probably disappointed her by not staying. Seems he was good at disappointing his mom. She didn't approve of his entrepreneurial zeal. She grew up in a generation where people worked at one place for their entire career. With that stability was the security of working for a reputable business. He always felt she didn't like that her son was a salesman, that somehow, it was a profession of loose morals and recklessness.

Was that really all his fault? He was doing the best he could. He always did the best he could. Yet, there he was disappointing his mother by not staying for leftovers and a blueberry buckle. Why couldn't she be happy with him? Look how hard he was working.

And now this. Fresh, new ideas. Isn't this what his father told him he needed to do? Have a plan for the future? Have new ideas? What was next? Isn't that what Dad wanted to know?

He stood up, stretched his back in an arch, shook out his arms. At the conference room window, he looked out on Manhattan. As usual, the streets were busy, loaded with pedestrians, taxis, and a smattering of other cars. Where were they going? Shopping, of course. Hopefully to stores selling his Airwaves. Though some were probably heading out for an early bite before a show. Erika loved the post-Thanksgiving shows. The energy of the audience was always much better, she'd said. He never understood what she meant.

Yeah, they weren't in sync.

It would be nice to have a partner to be in sync with right now. Someone climbing the mountain of success with him, supporting him. Someone, maybe like Amanda Hollingsworth—now there's a woman who obviously understood hard work.

Turning back around, he surveyed the messy papers scattered over the conference room table. He should get back to it. Compile lists of hotels, colleges, large companies. Oh, convenience stores. How many convenience stores now served quickly prepared foods?

He sat down at the table, pulled his laptop closer and started researching. He had staff who could be doing this, and stupidly he gave today off—paid—for the holiday. That was ridiculous. Who needed four days to celebrate Thanksgiving? He wouldn't make this mistake again next year.

Hours later, Patrick realized his neck resisted moving. He stood again, twisted it side to side, then stretched so his shoulders moved towards his ears, going back and forth until his neck loosened up. He rolled his shoulders. Man, he was tight. How long had he been staring at his computer? The clock showed it was just past seven. The long day was well worth the effort, though he was hungry again. The thought of more vending machine food was almost enough to forgo eating. Instead, he pulled out his cell and ordered up Chinese food. He'd eat, then finish organizing his design notes and ideas for expansion. He'd have to talk to his team first thing on Monday. Get them fired up for massive growth. This was it, a real light at the end of the tunnel.

He stared at his reflection in the windows as he resumed stretching. Couldn't let his back get stiff like that. That would be bad for his golf game. Thinking about that, he checked the weather app on his phone. *Low 60s tomorrow, clear skies.*

Perfect.

He sent a group text to his golfing buddies. *Anyone up for a round tomorrow?*

One by one, they all declined. Everyone was busy with family.

He almost texted back to check on Sunday, and then he changed his mind. He'd probably just get the same answers. He always spent the Saturday after Thanksgiving at his parents' club, playing golf with his dad if the weather was good enough before meeting up with old high school friends for a drink. Then Sunday, another final feast with his parents and a few neighbors—his little family's tradition—before he'd pack up and head back to his apartment.

A text shook him out of his memories. His food delivery was waiting for him at the office door.

He accepted his sweet and spicy General Tso's chicken and returned to the conference room. It didn't seem right that he was alone. He was used to it, though. As an only child, he used to be a little curious about his friends with big families. What was that like? Brothers and sisters arguing all the time, trying to assert dominance? Or was it supportive and loving, always doing things together?

Looking back, he realized it didn't bother him. He'd kept busy, doing things, accomplishing things. Everything

he'd set his mind to, he achieved. He didn't get bored. He could figure things out on his own. Meaning and purpose could be found through achievement and work. He could put his mind into whatever he chose.

Maybe that was partly because he had no siblings to distract him or, as he'd witness in other families, put him down or tease him. He grew up thinking he could do or be anything. So far, he'd proven himself correct.

If only he could figure out what to do or be in order for his parents to be proud. For mom, it was to be kind to everyone and treat them like family. For dad, it was to be the best he could be and treat everyone like he wanted to be treated. They were both big role models of integrity and humility, people to be esteemed because they did what they said they would do and didn't show off. They never talked about money being an important barometer for measuring success, yet they had plenty and Patrick needed it to keep making progress in the family. That was probably just a matter of time.

And then there was the relationship status, though it sure would be good to have someone to go home to at the end of a long day like today. Maybe even good to have a child or two running up to him, happy to see him. It was the great unknown and that made it both exciting and scary. It was the only thing that conjured up uncertainty. What if he didn't get married and have kids? Would it be something he would regret? The first step would be a relationship. So far, none of those had worked out. Erika may have been "the one", yet she couldn't see all that he was trying to do

for her. Every relationship had ended the same way, with a wonderful woman leaving because she didn't feel heard or understood. Oh well, he thought. Time was on his side. He was young, attractive, and moving up the success track every year. Be patient. Guys like me get the girl in the end.

He'd think about relationships later.

"Oh, Mr. Armstrong."

Patrick realized he'd been staring into an empty takeout carton and now he was no longer alone. The cleaning lady had arrived.

"We didn't expect to see anyone in here tonight."

"Just burning a little midnight oil." He stood up and started clearing the conference table. "I'll be out of your way in no time."

"Take your time, we'll start with the rest of the office." She smiled at him. "Did you have a nice Thanksgiving meal?"

"I did. I spent the evening with my parents in Connecticut."

"Lovely. I'm sure they were delighted to see you."

"Hmmm." He stacked his papers and tapped their ends on the table to line them up.

"So, are you going home now?" She gathered his food trash.

He watched her pick up after him as he mulled over the question. He really didn't want to go home to a dark apartment—to a place where all he'd have to do was stare at the television for entertainment.

He could continue working. While that had modest

appeal, he knew he needed to get his crew up to date first on everything he'd done that day.

"I don't know," he finally told her.

Chapter 5

"I don't understand," his mother's voice coming through the phone almost pained him. "It's the twenty-third of December. Why do you have to meet a client so close to Christmas? It can't wait until afterward?"

"I'm sorry, Mom." Patrick pinched the bridge of his nose and closed his eyes against the merry scene of Manhattan decked out for the holidays on the street below him. He'd never really lied to his parents before. Hated doing it now, especially with his mother sounding so . . . so hurt. "The guy's in San Francisco only for another couple of days before he flies home to Australia. He's holding up his trip home to meet with me."

"I guess I understand. You know your father and I are off to spend New Year's in the British Virgin Islands."

"Right, on the Bryant's yacht." Man, his parents had the life. Friends with yachts in the Caribbean for winter holidays. He'd be like that one day. It was just a matter of time. He was on the path: success, money, status . . . achievement. When he got there, he'd invite his parents to his own yacht. They'd be so proud. "That will be an amazing time for you and Dad. Look, our company holiday party is happening now. I'm already late. I hate to cut this short—"

"I understand. You're the head. You need to be there with your team members."

Yes. She acknowledged he had a company. And thankfully, she must have sensed he didn't want to talk to his father. He didn't want to face him, not yet. Not until he solidified the plan he had in place and lined up manufacturing for the new products. He needed to get to the party. Talk to Nico and Thad before everyone went home for the long holiday weekend.

He gave the taxi driver the address to the Happiest Hour. He'd never heard of the venue before and hoped it lived up to his assistant's gushing description. A little Miami in the heart of NYC, she'd called it.

"It's so kitschy. It'll be fun," she said. Then she snarled, "I mean, since you totally vetoed the Skylark."

He needed a new assistant. He should put that on his list. Emily was good at what she did, she just didn't seem to have the drive that he'd want in an assistant. She was happy to go home at five o'clock every day and leave things undone until tomorrow.

Though after stepping foot into the Happiest Hour, where his sense of aesthetics made it difficult not to turn around and run back out, he couldn't help wondering if letting Emily plan it at the Skylark was a better idea. The place was decorated with cartoon palm trees on the wallpaper, and an abundance of pink plastic flamingos and knick-knacks that looked like the ones his maternal grandparents had collected back in the 1950s when they went to Florida to vacation.

He'd only vetoed the Skylark because it was Erika's supposed favorite place. Erika. He hadn't thought about her since Thanksgiving and doing so now brought down his mood a little. He took his time getting used to the loud country-rock song playing in the background to collect his thoughts. He was still glad Erika had moved on. That had freed him up to focus on his business. Really, the breakup was one of the best things that had ever happened to him. In fact, every break-up he'd ever faced had been for the better. He'd grown through every one of them. He thought he must've found "the one" a half-dozen times and then, time after time, none had the understanding that matched what he had about doing what it takes to be successful.

Though it sure would be cool to be walking into this crazy place with a beautiful woman by his side. He wanted to share in the excitement of kicking off the New Year with high hopes for his company.

The hostess led him to the downstairs lounge area, a twenty-first century speakeasy affectionately called Slowly Shirley. The party was in full swing. Classic rock played in the background, and Patrick appreciated the more sophisticated vibe of the Art Deco decor. His team seemed happy—lots of smiling faces. He spotted Nico, looking like he was in a deep conversation with a woman who must be his date and two other team members. Patrick headed toward him, intent on talking to the man about the number of returns a retailer in Cleveland had.

Thad intercepted him. "You need a drink, my man." Thad slapped him on the back. "I can see it all over your face."

"What are you talking about?" Though a drink did sound good. Patrick let his CFO walk him over to the bar.

Thad ordered a complicated-sounding drink made with tequila, gin, blood orange, and other ingredients Patrick had never heard of. He watched the bartender, in a burgundy velvet jacket and bow tie do some magic. The man moved like an artist. How much was he spending on this party? There were too many ingredients in that drink.

"I think I need to reign Emily in next year," he told Thad as he accepted his drink. "This party is a little over-the-top."

"Patrick, your team is one of the hardest-working ones I know. We've all been burning the candles at both ends since that trade show in October. They deserve a good party—and good bonuses, which I happen to know Strong Appliances can afford."

"Seems to me their bonuses could be bigger if we weren't having such a swanky party." He sipped his concoction. Whew. That was quite the burn sliding down his esophagus. Another sip assured him it was worth the pain. What a delicious drink.

"Money isn't the only thing your team members want." Thad clinked Patrick's glass with his own. "They want the recognition that they did a good job. They need to see that there is light ahead at the end of this work-hard tunnel."

"What do you mean?"

"The other side of the phrase is 'play hard,' right? Work hard, play hard. It all has to balance."

"We're building an empire, Thad." Another sip. "Once it's built, they can play all we want."

"Let's hope the workers can make it that long." Thad turned and walked away, leaving Patrick alone with his drink and thoughts. The team were all having a good time, yet no one seemed too keen on checking in with him, coming over to chit chat. Their big smiles were aimed at each other, at their dates, at the bartenders. As if they didn't have a care in the world.

Was he the only one who understood how pivotal this time was? He was giving them all the next day, Christmas Eve, off. Many were taking vacation time the following week and not returning until January. Not him. There was so much to do to get ready for the New Year.

#

Having learned his lesson on Black Friday, Patrick entered his office suite on Christmas Eve loaded with shopping bags of food, bottles of water, a yoga mat, and resistance bands. He'd set a timer to make sure he stretched and got in a couple of short workouts. No need to let his health deteriorate while he was building an empire.

Once more he set up shop in the conference room. His goal was to review all the contracts in place and get them set up for renewal in the next year—renewal with an increase in expected orders.

Nico should have been there with him. He had all the intel on all the clients. Technically, reviewing the contracts was under his domain as part of his job. In theory, these contracts would be reviewed and summarized for Patrick, so all he had to do was give approval. Nico only laughed and patted Patrick on the back last night when he tried to talk to him.

"Careful, Patrick," Nico grinned. "We'll start calling you Scrooge."

"What do you mean? I'm paying everyone in this room very well."

"Not Scrooge, Nico," Emily chimed in. "Grinch. He's the one who didn't want people to enjoy their Christmas."

"Right," Nico belted out another laugh. "Patrick, everyone put in one heck of a year. You did, too. Give us all, including yourself, a night to relax and enjoy the holidays. We had a great run of it this past year. I promise you I'll have those contracts reviewed and ready for your approval by the end of the first week in January, in time for my deadline. Right now, it's party time. We all deserve a little respite and good cheer."

There were enough people clamoring *Yes, Cheers,* and even *Amen,* that Patrick let it go. He understood their need for a break. And, reluctantly, he had a good time at the party. The food was better than he'd expected, the complicated cocktails were amazing. Next year, they'd do a bigger one. His success, Strong Appliance's success, will be solidified. He'll be able to rest on his laurels. Maybe by then, he'll have achieved enough he'll have a date on his arm.

A sense of feeling alone, very alone descended on Patrick in the conference room. He stared at his laptop monitor, unable to clearly see the lines listing his clients in the database. Yes, everyone deserved to rest up after a year of hard work. Everyone deserved to enjoy a bit of holiday

cheer with loved ones. He did, too. He didn't have time for it this year. There were times a man just needed to make some sacrifices. Now was one of them for him.

He'd get a jump start on the contracts. Get all the easy ones out of the way and leave the more time-consuming ones to Nico when he returned after the New Year.

How could he approve anyone taking the entire week between Christmas and New Year off? He'd have to review that policy. This would be an important week every year.

He got himself a fresh cup of coffee and started in on the contracts.

It didn't take long for Patrick to discover things weren't as good as he'd expected. In fact, there seemed to be a number of retailers wanting new terms on their contracts, some seemed hesitant to renew.

What was going on? Clicking into their accounts, he found there were numerous complaints about delivery schedules and the quality of his Airwaves. Oh, no. Home Life didn't want to renew at all. How was that possible? And who authorized such a large refund for them? Thad.

He called Thad's cell number.

"Patrick, you all right?" Judging by the background noise on Thad's end, there were numerous people around him.

"I'm fine. The Home Life contract isn't." Patrick didn't bother to keep the annoyance out of his voice. "What is going on with that?"

"It's on our schedule to discuss after the New Year—"

"And we have the luxury to wait that long?"

"The new contract won't go into effect until the beginning of Q2, so yes, we have the luxury to wait a couple of weeks to discuss. Nico and I have been in constant contact with their buyers."

"And you haven't included me?"

"It's our job, Patrick. I didn't realize you felt the need to micromanage us. I thought you could trust us to do what we are supposed to do. Trust me. We have it under control. Strong Appliances will not lose Home Life."

"Daddy, it's your turn to squeeze the oranges," a little girl hollered in the background.

"Look, Patrick. It's Christmas Eve. Mine and my wife's families are all here. We have a tradition of everyone chipping in to make fresh orange juice. I need to go."

"Right." Patrick clicked off.

He supposed Thad had a point—he should be able to trust him and Nico to do their jobs. And he wasn't trying to micromanage anyone. It was just a shock to see this many complaints about his products. Why hadn't anyone told him?

He clicked into his team messaging app. There were numerous notes from Nico and Thad beginning with "heads up, we need to talk about . . ." or "let's review . . ." Patrick had given them a *thumbs up* or quick reply. They were all accounts he thought he had in the bag and were nothing to worry about. Clearly Nico and Thad weren't communicating things well enough. He'd need to set new expectations next year.

#

Christmas eve and Christmas day passed by in a haze of taking notes on deals that went sour and on retailers that were less than happy with Strong Appliances. There were enough complaints that Patrick started to waiver in his faith in himself. Perhaps his father was right. Maybe he should have sold this idea to a larger company. A place with secure connections to trustworthy manufacturers.

He spent the weekend researching manufacturers and Googling everything he could to learn about how other manufacturers handled quality control from half-way around the world. Being alone in his apartment felt smothering, so he continued going into the office, even though the echo of his footsteps on the marble floors seemed to emphasize how alone and isolated he was. Though he was still glad he chose not to spend the holiday with his parents. Having to spend four days with his father questioning everything he did would have been unbearable. Once he secured all his processes, he'd be happy to talk to Dad about it all. Once he secured his success.

What a relief that during the last week of the year, there were people who actually remembered they had jobs. He could hear the voices of a smattering of employees out in their cubicles, taking calls about warranties, replying to vendors, and tending to the other day-to-day necessities of keeping the business running. Their presence helped lift Patrick's mood a little. And boy was he happy to meet with Marissa from the marketing firm.

"The CES Conference is very influential," Marissa beamed across the conference table. "Your booth there

will help solidify Strong Appliances among the tech elite. Here's what we put together for you. It's a full package of pamphlets, testimonials, and statistics."

Patrick loved it all. He knew they'd have a great event at CES. The signage, the video they'd play in their booth, the other marketing products were all amazing. Yes. This was exactly the way he wanted Strong Appliances to look. He was going to wow the attendees. This was his chance to introduce his company as a rising star in the smart home category. His Airwave was already innovative and was only getting better.

As soon as he finished working out the bugs with the manufacturer. He just needed to take that off of Nico's plate. He'd handle it.

As soon as Marissa left, he dialed Thad.

"Patrick," Thad didn't sound happy to hear from him. "Look, I haven't seen my sister and her husband in person for over a year. We're out ice skating with our children at the Rock. Is this important?"

"I thought you'd like to know that I've just finalized the details for our booth at CES."

"Great."

"You realize that conference can make or break us, right?"

"I do."

Patrick was stunned for a heartbeat. "Are you telling me we need to button up our manufacturing issues before then? I've been researching other facilities. There is a significant cost difference, that I'd like to discuss with you."

"I'm coming, sweetheart. Ask Aunt Jamie to tie your skate." Thad's voice rose an octave while he spoke to what Patrick assumed was his daughter. Then it dropped when he returned his focus to the call. "There are two more days left in my vacation, Patrick. We can go over the numbers when I return."

"Gotcha." Patrick ended the call. All he needed was about fifteen minutes of his time. Maybe a little more. What was up with Thad?

Patrick didn't need to wait much longer to find out what was up with Thad. On New Year's Eve, as Patrick was in his office crunching numbers to compare manufacturing costs from different companies, an email from Thad slid into his Inbox.

Patrick:

I know this isn't the kind of email you like to read, and honestly, I'd rather tell you this in person, but since it also needs to be in writing, here it is. I'm resigning from my position at Strong Appliances effective January 31. I'm taking a new job beginning in February that will allow me to have more of a home-life balance. I simply need to spend more time with my wife, kids, and the rest of my family. You will have my full cooperation this month to help you find my replacement, get them up to speed, and help you on your trajectory toward success in whatever fashion that word means for you.

Wow, that wasn't anything Patrick would have ever predicted. He sat, stunned for a few minutes. It was long past five o'clock, in fact, when he glanced at his watch, he realized it was close to eleven at night. He was completely alone in his suite of offices. His beautiful suite of offices, part of the proof that he was building an empire, seemed unappreciated by everyone except himself at the moment.

He stood, approached the window, and pressed his face against the glass so he could look out into the black night sky above, then down into the bright lights of the city, still in her holiday glory.

Losing Thad was big. Very big. Maybe it was for the best. No, it was definitely for the best. Things always work out if you keep trying, right? He'd been slow coming to the realization that Thad wasn't quite the right person for the job, anyway. Similar to how Erika wasn't in sync with him personally, Thad didn't seem to be in sync with Patrick's professional drive. He'd have to find a new CFO as willing to roll up his sleeves as he was.

With that, he turned, packed up his belongings for the night and headed outside. Revelry throughout the city was hard to miss. Choruses of voices and blasts of music seemed to bombard him from every direction.

The closer he got to his apartment, the less eager he was to actually be in it. Instead, he ducked into a bar just a few blocks away. It, too, was filled with revelers. Patrick noticed they all seemed to have come in pairs: couples out ringing in the New Year together. No doubt intent on having that famous New Year's kiss.

He took a stool by the bar, near the back, not really wanting the free glass of champagne the bartender offered

him. He took it anyway. It would help pass the time until his real drink came.

Patrick sipped, found it difficult to keep a straight back. Everyone around him seemed too happy, so contented. Did they have a successful company behind their names? Were they building an empire? None of them seemed to even care about anything except this very minute, smiling and cheering with the person they loved. He let himself slouch, feeling an unbearable weight trying to crush him. Why was he alone? Why didn't he even have a friend here?

Who would that be? His golf buddies were . . . well, buddies. He thought about the times they'd sit at the "nineteenth hole" and have a drink at the end of the round. They talked about the game, whatever professional sport was in season, and about their business. Occasionally, one of them would mention their wife or make a joke about their family. Never anything below the surface. He couldn't call them friends . . . if they were, wouldn't one of them have invited him to a New Year's Eve party?

What about his college friends? Where were they? Well, he hadn't really kept in touch with them. He'd been too busy.

Now, feeling distant from his parents, with no woman in his life, no real friends, he was bringing in the New Year, the most hopeful and optimistic night of the year, alone and lonely.

Chapter 6

"I got it, Patrick." Nico's voice was clearly annoyed. "You've mentioned that already, several times." Nico shut his laptop and stuffed it into the backpack he used as an attaché.

"Sorry. Don't mean to be annoying." Though Patrick silently admitted to himself *he* was the one who deserved to be annoyed. He didn't quite approve of all the compromises Nico suggested were necessary to keep his retail clients happy. Yes, he knew Nico was right. What annoyed him was that they had to make the compromises. It wasn't his fault his manufacturer started using inferior parts and that the delivery terms changed mid-year with the freight companies. Why did his company have to eat all those expenses? "And in the end, what really matters is that we didn't lose any clients." Patrick stood from the conference table and stretched his back.

"That's the Patrick attitude."

"What do you mean?"

"Thank you for returning to being the eternal optimist."

"Returning?"

"Sometimes you forget that perspective and . . ."

"And what?"

"And, well." Nico stood slowly and pushed his chair under the conference room table. "Look, Patrick. I've been with you since the start, right?"

Patrick nodded.

"One of the things I loved about this company was your undying confidence, how sure you were about the product and the company doing great things."

"I'm still confident and sure."

"I know you are, it's just that sometimes you translate that into you taking over or not respecting boundaries."

"You're talking about Thad."

"I'm talking about everyone." Nico slung his backpack over his shoulder. "Seriously, Patrick. I know you're creating the next great thing here. However, the constant drive to go go go. It can lead to burnout."

"It's tough, Nico. I've always lived this way." Patrick shrugged. "Success. Achievement. That is what fuels my life."

"I can see that." Nico headed toward the conference room door, opened it and stopped. "Though Patrick, one day you'll burnout too if you're not careful. I hope while we're in Vegas for CES you let yourself take a few minutes to breathe and relax."

"Are you kidding me?" Patrick powered down his laptop. "I almost thought about tagging on an extra day to get in a round of golf. While I'm there, I intend to land at least six new accounts at CES. I'm going to need to get on a plane back home and kick out contracts with them right away."

"Did it ever occur that your new clients might be taking a few extra days in Vegas too?"

"Oh." Patrick stood upright. "Maybe I should stay an extra day. Maybe I could arrange for meetings with them."

Nico shook his head. "That's not exactly what I meant. Patrick, you do you." He slipped out the conference room door, leaving Patrick confused. What else could he have meant?

# # #

The temps hovered around sixty degrees when Patrick landed in Vegas. While not quite the warmth he was hoping for, at least it was better than the cold and rainy weather he'd left behind in New York. He waited at the baggage carousel with Nico and a few of his sales team members. They were all engrossed on their cell phones, presumably texting and calling people back home, assuring them they landed safely. He realized he should check in with his parents soon. They'd be getting back from their cruise while he was in Vegas.

A man next to him reached for a bag of golf clubs on the carousel.

"Here for golf?" Patrick asked him. "I've never played out here."

"Nah, I'm here for a conference." The man met his eyes. "I don't like to gamble. I thought I'd head out on the course after it's done to give my head time and space to clear. Know what I mean?"

"Yeah. Yeah, do I ever . . ." Patrick waved his hand in front of his face. Yeah, he finally knew what Nico meant, too. Maybe next year he would plan things differently.

He'd be more settled with the company, more secure with its success; then he'd be able to relax and play a round or two of golf.

Meanwhile, he had a conference to attend. Not just attend; a conference where he was going to show the movers and shakers in the smart home technology industry that he was a key figure among them. That was all he was going to focus on—make Strong Appliances a shining star.

"Let's go," he shouted, startling his team members. "Let's take over the world!" Beginning with six new accounts. Yes. He was landing six new accounts over the next four days.

#

Marissa and her marketing company really did wonders. Patrick stood in front of his booth and took a shot of his team at the ready standing behind it.

"Here," a woman with a CES name tag hanging from her neck approached him. "Get with your team, I'll take pictures of you all together."

"Thank you." Already, the day was off to a rocking start before the show was even open.

She insisted on taking serious and silly shots, which amped up his crew and helped everyone have genuine smiles on their faces and a can-do attitude by the time to the doors opened and attendees started streaming in.

"Nico," Patrick tapped his sales lead on the arm. "Here's what I think—"

"Patrick." Nico paused and raised his eyebrows. "Man,

you hired me because you thought I knew how to do my job. I can't if you keep trying to tell me how to do it."

"I just want this day to be successful." Patrick took a step backward, held his hands up in front of him, as if a police officer were pointing a gun toward him. "I'm not saying you can't do your job."

"Got it. And why don't we try letting it be successful instead of forcing it, eh?" Nico grinned and nodded. Patrick turned around. Their first visitor to their booth was here. "There are times good things happen when we simply let them—when we're not expecting them. When we constantly control how things work, we don't let that good stuff in."

Patrick wasn't sure about Nico's laissez-faire attitude. He dropped the subject though to avoid killing anyone's motivation or drive. Thankfully, it only took an hour for Patrick to feel confident that Nico really did know his stuff, as did the whole sales team. That meant he was free to do a little reconnaissance. Promising everyone he'd be back in the afternoon, he took off to wander through the exhibitor floor.

Meeting his competition was more fun than he'd anticipated. Instead of feeling inferior or that perhaps he was there too soon, he realized he was among like folk. Everyone was jazzed up and excited about the potential for business growth and what they could do to improve on whatever came before them. Every doubt about whether he should be in this sphere dropped from him as he rubbed shoulders with people younger, older, less experienced, and more experienced than he was—all treating him with

respect and appreciation. They were equally glad to be in his company as he in theirs.

He followed through on his promise to his team and returned to the booth later in the afternoon. They were rocking it. They'd landed a small retailer from Canada and managed to get the attention of Rasia Patel, the head procurement officer of one of the world's largest hoteliers.

"They're looking to upgrade their full-suite properties," Nico explained to Patrick. "Rasia wants to hear from you next week. She'd like to set up a time to chat and talk about how we can partner with them and bring custom-designed Airwaves to their properties."

"That's amazing." Patrick pulled Nico into a hug. He'd never done that before, never been that emotional with a team member. This was the best news yet. "Man, I am so proud of you. This is awesome. I'm not waiting until next week, though. I'm going to try to connect with her while we're here. Why not—"

"Give her a chance to get herself re-organized and settled back into a mental mindset for a decent conversation? In other words, why not wait until next week? There is no one here that has what we do. She's not going to find another provider. Give her space. We don't want her to think we're vultures waiting to pounce on a kill."

"Vultures don't pounce," Patrick said with a grin. "I get the point though. You know how I am."

"Perpetually driven, yeah."

# # #

Patrick didn't spend any time lounging around that evening or going out for a show or party with the others. He spent the evening eating from the room service menu and typing up all his notes from what he'd learned about his competitors and others at the show. There were tons of ideas, many new products out there, so much innovation. He wanted to stay abreast of it all. His dad may have been right about that; he needed to keep thinking about what to do for future growth.

Intending to spend the second day at the show the way he did the first, Patrick worked the booth with his team for an hour before heading out onto the floor. Not only did he want to visit booths in the other fields outside the smart home category; he wanted to attend a panel discussion on product placement. He was sure he could learn from that. He hadn't thought about product placement before, not until he'd spoken to one of his competitors yesterday who said sales of their vintage-inspired tea kettles with built-in water filtration took off after viewers saw it being used in a Netflix docudrama.

Surely, the Airwave could fit nicely on the set of a movie or television show. How many of those were set in homes? There had to be hundreds, if not thousands. Imagine if his Airwave landed in a designer kitchen of one of the hottest must-see shows? His parents would be knocked off their feet. And finally, Aunt Becky would be interested.

He grabbed a handout about the panel and found his way to a seat near the front. Within a few minutes, the moderator began introducing the three panelists who'd

speak and take questions from the audience. Patrick barely even noticed two of the panelists. The third, however, was all he could see or hear in the universe for the entire discussion.

Kayla Hansley was her full name according to the moderator and handout. CFO for a product placement firm headquartered in Boston, she spoke about the different types of product placement: screen placement, script placement, and plot placement. She could have been speaking about the most boring cures for insomnia and Patrick would have still been as mesmerized. He hung on every word, longed for more people to ask questions directly to her just to keep her talking. She was a complete knock-out with her curly chestnut hair and liquid-green eyes, and she was articulate and intelligent. She had such an easy, genuine smile.

Patrick forgot all about his promise to return to the booth for an hour before the show ended. He needed to meet this woman face-to-face, get to know her better. A quick read of her bio in the panel brochure told him her firm also had offices in NYC. He wondered how frequently she visited his city, and how could he get her to come more often.

After the panel discussion ended, Patrick remained in his seat while everyone else threaded out the door. When the panelists finally stepped down from the dais, he approached the amazing Kayla.

"Excuse me," he started and froze. He couldn't ask her out. He was a total stranger to her. She'd think he was a bit of a creep or worse. Then the words tumbled out. "I'd love

to hear more about what your company can do. I'm Patrick Armstrong, owner and CEO of Strong Appliances. Could I buy you a drink?"

"That sounds lovely." Her eyes crinkled as she smiled at him. "If you don't mind, I know it's not blazing hot outside, so perhaps we could head to the bar by the pool? I'd like to get some fresh air."

Nico was right again. No, Nico was almost right. He'd said good things happened when you didn't try to force them. This wasn't good. This was great.

Chapter 7

Patrick landed back in New York a very happy man. His company had contracted with five new accounts while at CES. He'd wanted six, and that sixth one was a sure-fire bet. Rasia Patel had emailed him to let him know she looked forward to partnering with Strong Appliances to bring the Airwave into their line of all-suite properties. Of course, the icing on the cake was Kayla. Not only had he spent the last two days in Vegas wondering around the CES event, they'd had dinner together both evenings, talking late into the night.

They spoke about everything, too. Not just business. It felt strange. He'd let down his guard and even told her how he could never seem to fulfill his parents' expectations of him. She'd spoken about her relationship with her family. They were like instant best friends, and he wanted more.

He just wished she wanted more, too. She was easy going and affable. Maybe everyone felt like an instant best friend with her.

She came to New York the following week and worked out of her company's corporate offices and dropped in on Patrick at Strong's office suite.

"What a beautiful set up," she exclaimed as he showed

her around. "And that view." She stopped before a window. As if on command, the sun shone through the clouds. Usually dreary and gray in the winter after the holiday season had passed, Manhattan seemed to sparkle just for Kayla. "How can anybody concentrate when you have that view just outside the window?"

"You'll have to come back in the summer when there's actually a little green." Patrick laughed, hoping she'd be coming back every season. "Let's go into the conference room to talk. Would you like coffee?"

After he got Kayla settled in the conference room, he headed to the lounge to make the coffee. He made a quick pitstop and on his way back, asked Thad to join them. They settled around the conference table.

"Is this a Herman Miller original?" Kayla asked, knocking on the walnut wood table.

"It is." Patrick couldn't believe Kayla recognized it. "I almost bought one made for today with USBs and outlets built into them; then I couldn't resist this special one from the 1950s. And I liked the idea of taking the tech out of the conference room, where we're supposed to confer, after all."

"I love it." Kayla's green eyes sparkled while she laughed. "Such a warm touch. And I see you do have a laptop in here." She pointed to his laptop he'd left on a credenza earlier in the day.

"Guilty," he pointed to himself. "At times I do like to work in here." Which he really didn't want to do at the moment. He wanted to see her laugh again. Oh man, he

was smitten. He took a deep breath. He needed to focus. "This is Thad, my CFO, currently."

"Nice to meet you." Thad shook Kayla's hand before sitting in one of the green leather chairs. "I understand you have some ideas on how to help Strong grow?"

"I hope so." Kayla reached into her attaché and pulled out a binder. "It seems you are already poised for massive growth. I'm sure you're excited for what's ahead of you."

Thad looked directly at Patrick. "I'm excited to see where the company goes. I . . ." He cleared his throat. "Sadly, I will not be going there with them. I'm only here for a couple more weeks."

"Right, Thad has other big plans ahead of him." Patrick didn't want this conversation to spiral downward. The last thing he needed was for Thad to complain about how there was no work-life balance in front of Kayla. "And he's still providing valuable input while he's here, which is why I wanted him to review your ideas with me. And if you had questions specifically finance related, he'd be in a better position to answer them."

"Actually, Patrick knows everything I do." The way Thad said it almost sounded as if he were hinting at nefarious intent. Granted his attitude hadn't been the best since his resignation, and Patrick somewhat understood. He already had a foot out the door. The man promised to be a team player for the month.

"Right, well, Kayla. Let's see what you've got."

Kayla went through a full presentation. She had great ideas for getting his Airwave into product placements. She had great ideas for expanding into untapped markets—had he thought of contracting with the government? Military housing? Low-income housing that the states paid for? No. He hadn't thought of any of it.

"This . . . is all just amazing." He looked over at Thad. "You sure you want to leave this place? Look what we can do."

Thad laughed. "She drives a hard bargain, Patrick, however I already have new gig lined up."

"The question is, how do you proceed from here?" Kayla asked. "Thad, is there enough cash or can a credit line be secured to ramp up production if Patrick gets one of these contracts?"

"All of these contracts." Patrick corrected her, hoping to sound full of enthusiasm and eagerness while feeling far too close to the opposite. She had a point. Contracting with the military to provide Airwaves in base housing would be even bigger than an all-suite series of hotels. Could he manage that? Was he big enough for that? Was his company really *that* good? Look how he almost failed last year's retailers.

"Right, Patrick?" Thad asked him a question.

Patrick shook his head. "I'm sorry. I was, um . . . my mind was mulling over something else. Could you repeat that?"

"I said we have great allies in the banking industry. And now that the manufacturer agreed to refund us for switching out to shoddy supplies over last fall, we have a bit of a surplus of cash."

"Right." That's right. The manufacturer admitted to cutting corners that were in clear violation of the contract and promised to pay Strong Appliances for every refund they had to give to retailers. That was actually a good move Thad had made. He was the one who worked with the attorneys to get the manufacturer to do right by them. And frankly, Patrick felt more confidence in the manufacturer now. That refund negotiation was a move of strength. No one would try to undermine Strong Appliances again.

#

Kayla continued to visit Patrick each time she came to New York whether she was there for business with Strong or another client. Without even realizing what was happening, their meetings turned into dinners—evenings spent enjoying good food and drink, discussing a little business because Patrick just couldn't help himself, and a lot of everything else. Meanwhile, the trickle of applicants coming in for Thad's replacement left much to be desired. Shortly after Thad's last day, in early February Patrick suggested he and Kayla have dinner at Le Bernardin's.

"I'd love to. I've heard a lot about it. And seafood is my favorite." Could she be any more perfect?

"Then, how do you feel about ordering the chef's tasting menu?"

"That would be amazing. I've never experienced anything like that before." Apparently, she could be even more perfect.

"Wonderful. I'll make the reservations." Patrick hung up his phone almost tingling with excitement. He felt like a school kid when the cute girl whose locker was next to his smiled at him. Only this wasn't just a crush. He was falling for this woman.

Did he have time for a real relationship, though? Was he at a good point in his life? His company was poised for massive growth, he made a great living . . . did that mean he was there? He was advancing rapidly in his business and could handle it. Of course he could. As one advances in business, they grow and are capable of handling more. In relationships, this time would be different. This was a business woman who understood him and had seen him in action. She was still interested in him.

He'd found the right woman. He was so close to big level-up. Everything had been leading up to this point in time. He was so excited to finally make it happen.

And Thad was gone. He had to take over his role, at least for a little while longer. It wasn't just a matter of did he have the time. Would he have the energy? The ability to focus?

Of course, all this could be a moot point. Kayla hadn't exactly said she was wildly in love with him or anything. They were simply two adults who enjoyed each other's company.

Two single adults . . .

One male and one female, single adults . . .

One seriously infatuated male and one . . . female who could have any man she wanted. She was beautiful, smart,

and articulate. Surely, she'd rather be with a man who already had made it, not one on the way.

He needed to stop thinking about this. There were still a few hours before dinner. It was too late to get a reservation, however he'd been there often enough, and he knew Charles could squeeze him in.

That would impress her, right? He was a regular at one of the top restaurants in New York City. Certainly, that meant he was someone special. Why couldn't he ask Kayla for more of a relationship?

# # #

Charles was, indeed, able to do his magic. He set Patrick and Kayla up at an intimate corner table. Kayla's eyes appeared to reflect every shiny object and light in the room. She seemed dazzled. Yes, Patrick did right by bringing her here.

Charles seemed to sense this was a special occasion because as soon as the waiter took their order, he returned to the table.

"You're going to love the tasting menu tonight," he told them. "To make it even more special, Chef Eric himself will be out within a few minutes to tell you about it."

A small gasp escaped Kayla. She quickly covered her mouth with her hand, and her cheeks reddened. "I can't believe I just made that noise. This is all very exciting to me. Is this normal for you?"

"No," Patrick, too, was stunned by the surprise. He'd

heard rumors that the famed chef often came out and spoke to the patrons, yet he never did it when Patrick dined there. Surely this was a good sign of things going his way. "I'm just as excited as you."

Soon enough, Chef Eric approached their table and introduced himself. "We will begin tonight with Taragai. Are you familiar with it?"

Patrick nodded and Kayla shook her head. Chef Eric went on to explain the various dishes and the chosen wines to go with them. Kayla was so delightful to watch as he spoke. Clearly, she enjoyed what was happening. Patrick only wanted that to increase throughout the evening.

"I cannot believe what's about to happen," Kayla said after the chef left the table.

"It does sound pretty amazing." Patrick smiled into her eyes. "We're off to a great night tonight." He picked up his wine glass for a toast.

She picked hers up as well. "Here's to . . .?"

"A great night."

They sipped.

"Let's get the business stuff out of the way." Kayla adjusted her napkin on her lap. "Then we can just have a night of fun. How's that sound?"

"Well, if it's good business stuff, then it will be fun for me. What's up?"

"It is good. We've secured product placement of the Airwave in a family sitcom that starts filming this summer."

"Really? That's amazing."

"Yes. I heard back from the producer's office as I was

wrapping things up this afternoon. I'm so glad I could tell you in person."

"I am, too." This night was one for the records. It would only be made better if he could get Kayla to agree to move to New York. He wanted to see her more. Especially now that Thad was gone, and he had less time. Wait a minute. "You know, Kayla, I am beyond impressed with you."

She laughed. "I enjoy what I do. It's easy to get good results when you have fun with your job."

That was an interesting concept. One Patrick hadn't really thought of before. Maybe he'll noodle on it later when he had more time. "Well, I'm impressed with everything about you. Your work. Your enthusiasm for life. Your willingness to try the chef's tasting menu."

She laughed again. "How could I resist?"

"Well, here's another offer, hopefully you won't be able to resist."

Her face grew serious. She raised her eyebrows.

"What do you think of becoming the CFO of Strong Appliances."

Her face shifted. A small smile appeared, the exuberance from her eyes left. Patrick got the sense she was disappointed. "Um, well, thank you, Patrick." She gave a small nod. "The answer is no. I, um, I enjoy your personal company and I enjoy collaborating with your actual company. The reality is I do not want to work for you."

Patrick swallowed against a whoosh of nausea. Seemed like every moment of insecurity, every tortuous second he'd ever had of feeling rejected and failing washed through his

body in a hormonal acid bath. How could he have misread things? Why did he constantly disappoint the people he most wanted to impress?

Looking into her face, he realized he hadn't. She wasn't disappointed in him; she was disappointed in his ask. Frankly, so was he. Because it was the wrong thing to ask for.

He was at a pinnacle moment in his career. His empire was on solid ground. He was in his favorite restaurant with one of the most amazing women in the world. The freaking celebrity chef came out and spoke to them. He was the man. He could ask her the right question.

"Okay then." Patrick leaned over the table, cocked his head to the side and grinned. "If you won't work for me then you have to marry me."

The twinkle returned to her eyes as she laughed once more. "Are you serious?"

Patrick nodded. "As serious as I've ever been." He stretched a hand over the table. Kayla reached out and placed her in it.

"Then I guess I have to marry you, Patrick Armstrong."

# # #

"Two months. You're getting married in two months?" His mother's voice was almost shrill over the phone.

"Yes. She's the perfect woman, Mom." Patrick spoke into his phone's speaker while he finished getting dressed for work. His first day as an engaged man. "Kayla will be moving from Boston to New York. She'll need to take care

of getting out of her lease and settling her affairs up there. Otherwise, we'd just do it now."

"How long have you known this woman?" Mom still didn't seem on board with the idea.

"Just—" Patrick paused in dressing as well as talking. No wonder Mom was kind of freaking out. He'd only known Kayla for a couple of months. "Look, I haven't known her long, Mom. We have this crazy bond. I know it. She knows it. We're in sync. Remember how I said Erika and I weren't in sync?"

"Yes."

"Well, Kayla and I are the opposite."

"That's great, son. I still don't understand the rush."

Neither did Patrick. He just understood this was the woman of his dreams, and he saw no reason to hold off being with her any longer than necessary. "I can't wait for you to meet her, Mom. You and, um, Dad." A stabbing pain of guilt hit Patrick. He hadn't laid eyes on his parents since that disastrous Thanksgiving meal. He'd make up for it. As soon as he hired a CFO. As soon as the company was stable in its growth. As soon as he knew his parents would finally approve of what he was doing.

Chapter 8

"Hi, um, Dad." Patrick cleared his throat and looked over at Kayla. She gave an encouraging nod, then tilted her head toward their son, Liam playing with his Thomas the Tank Engine train set his parents had given to him for his third birthday last week.

He knew Kayla was right to encourage him to reconnect with his father. She was much more in tune with what being a family meant than Patrick was. Kayla had proven to be a wonderful wife and an amazing mother. Her instincts kicked in the second they found out they were expecting Liam, who was due on their first anniversary. Her skills and natural ability only seemed to increase over the following two years. And, now in a constant beautiful glow of her pregnancy with a little girl, he ceded to her being the true leader in their family. Without question, she made decisions that guided the three of them along the best course for the highest good of them all. And she set the finest example of good judgment that any man—any father—could have.

When she'd first met his parents, she immediately picked up on the fact that Patrick and his father needed to have a closer relationship. She never harped on him, just gently brought it up as time went on. Then, with the birth

of their Liam, after his parent's ever-quick visit to meet their grandson, Kayla became insistent. She pointed out to Patrick how he had fallen in love fast and hard with his own son and asked point blank, "Doesn't your heart ache over the lack of relationship you have had with your own father? Surely, he must have felt that kind of love for you at one time. Maybe that's why he had such high expectations of you."

Patrick wasn't convinced. He and his father barely exchanged more than a nod hello the entire time they visited at Liam's birth and the subsequent rare family events. While that seeded resentment in him, it only made Kayla more resolute. Now that Liam was starting to ask questions, she felt it was unfair of them not to let him have a relationship with his grandfather. She'd called it a gift they'd give their children, and said Patrick was the key to making that gift happen.

"Is everything all right, son?" Dad brought him back to the present.

"Yeah." Patrick cleared his throat and walked over toward his playing Liam. "I, uh, well, I'm, well, I'm making arrangements to play in a golf tournament out at Pebble Beach."

"Nice. That should be a highlight of your golfing life."

"Yes, you know, it will be." He watched Liam's eyes light up as he pieced track parts together. "It's ultimately a fundraiser for, um, for kids with cancer."

"Always a good cause. Didn't know they held such events there. Good for them."

"Right." Why was this so hard? How is it he felt there was much more than just a few decades and seventy-five miles between them? How is it he could feel so close to his son that he wasn't sure where he ended and Liam began, and yet his father was alien to him? "Um, like, I need a golf partner, and . . .um . . ."

"Yes?"

He felt Kayla wrap her arms around his waist, hugging him from behind. Oh, how he appreciated her support and unconditional love.

"And, well, I thought it's been a long time since we played a round together. What do you think? Would you like to join me?"

"I'd never turn down a chance to swing a club at Pebble Beach."

Well, that was that. Dad was coming. Not because he wanted to be with Patrick. It was because Pebble Beach was such pull. Granted, Pebble Beach *was* one of those dream courses you never really expect to play. Really, he couldn't blame his father for that.

# # #

Patrick flew out to California seated next to his father in first class. They each had bought their own ticket, though Patrick really wanted to purchase both. That need, that constant pressure to do whatever he could to impress his father gnawed at him the entire flight out to the West Coast. They traveled in silence. His father reading the *New York Times* on his iPad. Patrick pretending to read sales reports

from his crew. He couldn't focus enough to make sense of the numbers in their rigid columns in a spreadsheet. He longed for his father to ask what he was looking at; he wanted to find a way to prove to him he was a success, that his father should be proud of him, that he could compete for his attention, and win, against the *New York Times*.

At least Patrick secured the rental car at the Monterey Airport. Surely Dad would approve of a Land Rover for them to travel to the resort at Pebble Beach. Dad didn't say anything about the SUV. He did, however, appreciate the view on the way down. Instead of taking the highway for the short ride to Pebble Beach, Patrick chose to go the slightly longer route along Jack's Peak. This way, they'd have the forested ridge to enjoy along the way.

"Ah, my favorite road in the country," Dad smiled as they turned onto famous 17-Mile Drive. "Though I've only seen it once."

"You played here before?" Patrick never heard his father mention that. Though he wouldn't be surprised. Of course, he'd played all the famous courses: St. Andrews in Scotland, Doral in Miami, even Elephant Hills in South Africa where he had to wait for a wart hog to leave the putting green before he could finish a hole. Dad was good. He could have been a pro. Patrick would never play as well as he could.

"So many years ago." Dad waved his hand in front of his face. "Before you were even born. Before I'd met your mother. I was here with your grandfather."

Patrick felt the wave of an emotion wash through him

that he couldn't identify, couldn't name. He just knew it felt uncomfortable. He cleared his throat.

"How was it?"

"Ha," Dad snorted a laugh. "I played horrible. My old man, though." He let out a whistle. "He could have been a pro."

Patrick's stomach churned. That unnamed feeling seemed to well up within him, a cross between sadness and anxiety. He didn't understand it, couldn't make himself speak though he longed to change the subject. Why couldn't Dad talk about the multi-million-dollar houses they were passing? Why not discuss the latest golf tournament on TV? Why not anything else?

"He really wanted me to attend Stanford, his alma mater." Dad paused. Patrick braved a quick glance over in time to see him run his hand through his thick white hair. "We flew out here to look at the campus. He hoped I'd fall in love with California enough that I'd want to go there. Part of that wooing was playing Pebble one day, Spanish Bay the next, and Spyglass the third. I barely remember anything about Stanford's college campus. I think I have an imprint of views from each of those courses forever etched in my brain. I returned to the East Coast completely lukewarm about California and madly in love with golf. My father was disappointed, to say the least."

"I never, um, knew that." Patrick choked out the words. He wished his father would change the subject. They didn't talk like this—they didn't talk about personal things. He wasn't sure how to respond or what to do about the

heavy sensation now on his chest. Suddenly, he questioned Kayla's suggestion. This week would have been much more fun if he'd asked one of his golf buddies to join him.

"Yeah, well, it was just one more thing we disagreed on. He wanted me to study architecture, just like he did. Then become a member of his firm and take over the company one day." Dad grew quiet. "I guess it's a father thing. When a man reaches a level of success and stability, he just wants his kids to have that, too. It's hard to watch them risk by taking another path."

Patrick had never enjoyed seeing a valet driver anywhere as much as he did the one who greeted him at the Lodge at Pebble Beach Resort. He needed that change of focus. He'd never heard his father talk about his grandfather like that. The two of them had always had a cold, almost estranged relationship as far back as Patrick could remember. His father's parents had passed away when he was very young. He didn't have the fun memories he did of his mother's parents. And the way Dad was talking . . . it almost sounded like he was extending an olive branch of sorts. Like he was trying to explain himself for wanting Patrick to . . .

Oh. A dawning realization came over Patrick as he approached the check-in desk. He'd always assumed Dad was hard on him because he expected Patrick to be better than he was at everything, to reach a level that Patrick seemed unable to reach. Yet it seemed as if Dad really just wanted Patrick to have a life that was as good as his. Could he have misread his father his entire life?

He wished Kayla was there with him to help him process this. She was much better at the emotional things. Meanwhile, he needed to get his game head on straight. He was about to play three rounds of golf at one of the most iconic courses in the world. If he was going to impress his dad on the links, he needed to start thinking like a champ.

It wasn't until after he'd checked in, placed his belongings in his room, and had walked out onto Terrace Lounge deck to sign in at the registration desk for the tournament that he realized he didn't have to work to impress his father. Dad had already registered and was staring out toward the eighteenth hole and the bay beyond. Such a peaceful, happy smile on his face. Dad wasn't here for Patrick to impress him. He was here for the experience, and already seemed impressed.

"Hey, Dad." Patrick placed a tentative hand on his father's shoulder. How long had it been since he'd touched the man? Touched him because he wanted to, not because he was obligated to hug him hello or goodbye? That almost-nauseating feeling overtook Patrick once again. Those same nameless sensations he'd felt cruising along 17-Mile Drive.

"Patrick. Look at this view." Dad spread his arm in front of him. "Isn't it magnificent?"

"You bet." And it was. The green was lush, the bay a deep, deep blue. There were even a few luxury yachts with lights on in the water.

"I hope you come out here with Liam and enjoy this place when he's old enough. I should have brought you out here."

"I will, Dad. You know I always try to live up to your expectations." Patrick squeezed his shoulder and dropped his hand. His dad had regrets? That was hard to fathom. The man was always confident, so sure he was doing everything right.

"Patrick." Dad turned toward him. The late-afternoon sun was at a low enough angle that it lit up the side of Dad's head, giving his white hair a golden hue.

Patrick noticed for the first time ever that his father was aging. In fact, there were enough creases on his face that others would call him an old man. When did that happen?

"Pat?" Dad's forehead wrinkled into a frown.

"Sorry, Dad. Just lost in thought. What's up?"

This time his father was silent a moment, as if he needed the mental space to figure out what he wanted to say. Patrick watched his face, feeling his stomach churn, his throat tighten. The name of the emotion was on the tip of his tongue.

"Patrick, I think I owe you a long-overdue, heartfelt apology." Dad's lips pressed together in a tight line. Patrick watched him take a long inhale.

"What for?" Patrick breathed deeply, too.

"I guess, well, I always wanted the best for you. For you to have as many advantages, as many good experiences, as possible. And for you to always feel safe, secure, and not want for anything." Again, Dad paused.

Patrick couldn't respond. His throat was paralyzed.

"It seems I wasn't good at expressing that. I guess I came across as setting unrealistic expectations on you. I

promise you son, they weren't expectations, they were hopes and dreams."

Patrick could only nod. Finally, he knew the name of the emotion using a battering ram to burst through his solar plexus: grief. He was grieving the relationship he'd always wanted with his dad and never had. Only now he realized what was blocking that relationship wasn't really anything his father had done. It was all about how he, Patrick, had interpreted it. He'd been blocking himself.

Meanwhile, his father was growing older, faster than Patrick ever thought possible. He, himself, was growing older too. He needed to do whatever he could to make up for all that lost time, all those lost connections—beginning now.

Patrick ripped his father into a tight hug. He felt the wetness in his eyes and sniffed.

"Listen, Dad." He let him go, wiped his face with his hands. "I appreciate you saying that. And you know what, maybe I needed to think you had higher than realistic expectations on me. I kind of think that's what helped me get to where I am now. I'm successful. I have the love of a good woman, my soul mate, who's the greatest wife and an excellent mother. And I'm here, on one of the most famous golf courses in the world about to play three rounds with my father. Don't think life can get any better, can it?"

"Well, you got one thing wrong, son." Dad grinned.

Patrick felt his legs weaken. "Really?"

Dad tapped his chest with a fingertip. "I'm the one who's married to the greatest wife."

"Ha," Patrick laughed. "Maybe we can we tie on that one?"

Dad laughed. "Deal. Now, let's find the Tap Room. I could handle a good steak and beer right now."

#

"Oh, Patrick, I'm very happy for you." Kayla's warm voice seemed to embrace him through the phone. "Sounds like you and your father really bonded."

"Yeah." Patrick leaned his forehead against the windowpane. At just after eight o'clock in the evening, the sun was near the horizon, tinting the Pacific in shades of orange, red, and purple. "Anyway, I won't keep you. I know it's late on the East Coast. I apologize for that. I just thought you'd be happy to know how today went."

"I'm glad you called. And I was up anyway. Ashley was just telling me I should have the strawberries."

"Ashley?"

Kayla laughed "Just trying the name on for size. I can't believe how much fruit I'm craving during this pregnancy."

Patrick couldn't believe that this time next year he'd have a son and a daughter. Two little people he'd be responsible for. Man, he hoped he wouldn't mess it up. He knew he'd figure it out.

"It's so good you'll be with him all weekend. You can start making up for lost time right away."

"Oh, I will. I just can't believe how fast things changed. All it took was a couple of sentences for me—for us—to

understand each other. It's crazy, Kayla. I'd spent most of this day in turmoil about my relationship with my father. Struggling to constantly do and say the right things. Not just this day, I think for most of my life. And it was all a misunderstanding. He didn't expect better for me, he just wanted the best for me. I can't believe I've wasted so much time in resentment over nothing." As he said this, a different feeling came over him. He had misinterpreted the intentions and feelings of his father. How had this happened? He was able to spot, with uncanny accuracy, what people were thinking. And this somehow slipped through his radar. Was it possible other things were undetected and unnoticed? It was possible, although unlikely. His ability to see others was honed and razor-sharp. Yet this most important relationship had caught him completely blind . . .

"That's done and over with," Kayla reminded him. "The important thing is that you two connected. Now, you just gotta focus on maintaining that connection. Keep it up. And . . ."

"And what?"

"And remember how it all began. You have a son of your own. I've already heard you mention things like how you can't wait to get him his first set of clubs and teach him how to golf, and that you want him to go to the same sleep-a-way camp you did when he's older, and—"

"Yeah, what Dad wouldn't want that for his son? I mean, if he's going to grow up and be successful, he'll want to play golf. Do you know how many deals are negotiated

out on the range? And camp is a must. No question my best people skills came from that camp."

"Right."

Yeah. He had the greatest wife ever. Kayla was so wise.

Chapter 9

"You don't look so good." His ever-blunt assistant, Emily, paused whatever she was doing at her computer and stared at Patrick as he headed into his office. "You all right?"

"I'm fine," Patrick laughed. "Better than ever, in fact. My dad and I had a great weekend in California. I'm a little jet lagged." He dumped his keys and cellphone onto his desk and headed to the breakroom.

"Nico, my man." Patrick slapped him on the back then paused in the middle of the room. He turned sideways, deliberately stepped his feet a little wider than shoulder-width, bent slightly at the waist, then mimed hitting a golf ball. "Some of the best rounds of my life."

"Awesome. Where'd you end up?" Nico poured him a cup of coffee.

"Just one back from second place."

"Not bad."

"Not at all, considering the two top teams had pros on them." Yeah, it was proof his dad could have been a pro. He was amazing to watch out on the course. Patrick couldn't have been prouder.

"And Kayla held up okay being a single mom?" Nico walked with him back toward his office.

"Of course. Kayla could rule the world as a single mom. Though I think it helped that her parents came up to stay with her. She took advantage of having two sets of helping hands and got much needed rest." She did look positively radiant when he came home. She was so beautiful, laughing with him over the bowl of strawberries in her hand.

The icing on the cake, though, was a moment he didn't feel comfortable sharing with Nico. It was his Dad hugging him—genuinely hugging him—and thanking him for one of the best weekends of his life before they parted ways at JFK airport. So much had changed in just the span of a couple of days.

"I put that proposal on your desk." Nico pointed his coffee cup through the open door of Patrick's office. "Hit me up after you review it. That's one of the largest state universities in the Midwest. They received several million from an alumnus specifically aimed at upgrading all their undergrad dorms and want to put Airwaves in each one."

"You are the man." Patrick almost spilled his coffee with his excitement. "I'll read it now." He headed into his office happier than he'd ever been in his life. A great time with his dad at a world-class golf resort. A happy Kayla. Last night he'd watched the first-ever prime-time television commercial for the Airwave and now this. A college university wanting Airwaves. Things couldn't get any better.

Nah, he knew they could get better. It was just a matter of expecting them to be that way.

His cell rang within seconds of taking a seat at his desk. Mom was calling.

"Hey there, Mom. What's up?" Patrick spun in his office chair to face his computer. He shook his mouse to bring his monitor to life.

"Oh, Patrick." Mom's voice was off. He froze.

"What, what is it?" He asked after a couple of heart beats.

"Your father . . . Patrick, you must come home. Right away."

"Why? What happened?" He was already standing again.

"Your father's had a stroke, Patrick. He's in Yale New Haven Hospital. I need you."

#

Patrick had to check himself as he drove to his hometown, to the hospital where his mother was waiting for him. He pressed the speed as much as he could, darting around other cars on the highway with precision, while trying not to draw the attention of the police. He *had* to get to his father. Dad *needed* him. He *needed* Dad. They had so many years of disconnect to make up for.

The drive that normally took a little over two hours, ended in just under.

Yet he was still too late.

He found his mother slumped over in a chair in the waiting room. A table housing empty coffee cups and a messy stack of magazines was on one side of her, a physician in pale green scrubs on the other. She held her face in her hands; the doctor's head was near hers, his hand on her back.

Without being close enough to hear, Patrick knew exactly what he was telling her. His father was gone.

He'd just connected to the man, finally, after a lifetime of being too far apart. And he was gone.

As if sensing his approach, his mother looked up. Her tear-stained face broke everything inside Patrick. He ran to her, pulled her into his arms, and cried into her shoulder. How could he have lost his father so soon after finding him? That was just wrong. Cruel.

#

The punishment continued as plans for the funeral rolled out. Patrick's parents, always the kind to prepare well, already had everything preplanned and prepaid. Caskets had been picked out. Eulogies and obituaries were written. A catering service showed up at the house and took care of putting out their foods while simultaneously accepting the various casseroles and meals brought by friends. It all happened as a result of just one phone call.

Never had Patrick felt so useless, so in the way, so . . . incompetent. He bumbled around and tried to blend in with the furniture. He hated interacting with all the people who showed up at his childhood home to tell him how wonderful his father was, how good of a man, how much he'll be missed.

Patrick didn't need to be told that. He knew it already. It was a truth he had denied himself for most of his life. Now that knowledge cut through him like a blade on fire. The pain was unbearable, crushing, debilitating. And there was nothing he could do about it. He could only feel it. Nothing to distract him from grieving a lifetime of missing out on what every child deserved—a relationship with their father.

Dad's good bourbon was a bit of a solace. Dad's library became his quiet place. Out of the way of all the guests, out of the line of sight of his mother's sad eyes, he was able to pour a couple fingers in a crystal glass and toast his dad. Once the burn in his throat subsided, it was easier to go out and pretend to pay attention to the guests. With a little help from that amber liquid, he could handle the nodding, the speaking softly, the feeling too much, while more and more people poured into the house. The bourbon helped numb the pain, block out the grief, and give him the wherewithal to stand upright through the viewings and final funeral service.

#

His mother wanted to stay in the house. It was much too big for just her now. Frankly, it had always been too big for their entire family. She didn't care. She loved it. She wanted to stay and after the funeral, he left her there and returned to his own little family's high-rise apartment in the city, promising to check in frequently, knowing Kayla would do it for him.

An emptiness had set up inside him during the week of services for his father. An emptiness that only got deeper with each passing day. Patrick realized whoever said time healed all wounds was wrong. Time healed nothing. Time only marked how long the wound lay open. He didn't seem capable of healing from his father's death at all. It was a battle on a field in which he was not trained.

He experienced an emotion that was truly terrifying for him. And there wasn't an obvious avenue to follow that could help him to resolve it. He found himself trembling with tears at the thought of his father. What scared him the most was that he couldn't easily control his feelings. He hadn't learned how to think his way through this one, not yet.

More practice, deal with it. You've got this. Mantras repeated in rapid succession to himself seemed to help in the moment. Still, the pain was lodged under the surface like a jagged splinter just out of reach. He could deal with it. There were other splinters of pain. This one, however, was different and tough to forget.

The only thing he could do was distract himself from the pain. Anytime he wasn't busy, anytime his brain didn't have a problem to solve, a challenge to meet, it seemed to slow down and take notice of the bitter ache that threatened to overtake his soul. Those rare moments when he wasn't working—at the end of the day when Kayla would want to spend a quiet evening at home with him, when alone in a hotel room waiting for night to fall so he could get up and get back to work the next day—the pain and emptiness would come flooding back in until the bourbon blocked it out. He could block it, but he hadn't figured out how to make it go away. The tears were less frequent although they were always there lying in wait.

He learned to drink enough to be numb when he wasn't working. It was a delicate balance. The feelings boiled inside him, and deep inside him knew it wasn't a healthy way of dealing with anything. He just didn't see any other way out. He could not share with Kayla. First, men don't burden their women with problems like this. He'd only seen his father cry one time ever in his whole life at his mother's funeral. He grew up learning to *deal with things* that made him want to cry. He didn't show tears to others. Women are not attracted to men who cry, and he wouldn't risk losing Kayla over this—not an option.

Should he share with his mother? She had cried enough and to see her son as a little boy crying—that would cement in her mind how immature he was. No. His time to cry had passed at the funeral. He barely remembered the day—it was a foggy haze, his memory unclear. One thing that was clear; he didn't cry.

Thank God there was work. A technological breakthrough fixed the European dilemma and now the mini Airwave could be produced for households on that continent. All he had to do was get buyers to find it interesting. No, they needed to find it intriguing. They needed to find it imperative to have in their lives.

Soon, there were marketers and publicists across the European continent to meet. Campaigns to be created. Retailers to be wooed. Manufacturers, warehouses, distributors . . . it was like at the beginning of the company. Only now there was the added complexity of needing interpreters and all the many different international laws and regulations to boggle his mind.

The airline frequent flyer miles added up, the hotel

points placed him in elite categories. And the empty bourbon bottles filled recycling bins. There was a raw energy fueling him as he found a sense of purpose again. His father would be so proud of him now. He truly was building an empire.

Like a shark, as long as he kept moving, he felt alive. The deals, the travel, the meetings, the marketing campaigns, the strategies, the new people and new places—it all fueled his forward motion through life. Those times when he had to stop, he felt as if he were drowning.

Kayla was left to manage the home life details, which she did with grace and efficiency. Though as her pregnancy progressed, she seemed to want more from him. She wanted him at home more. She wanted him to help her practice the breathing exercises for the birth. She wanted him to sit quietly with her in the evenings, to place his hand on her abdomen and wait to feel their little girl to move.

There were times when slowing down and snuggling with his wife on the sofa did seem like what he needed. Just not at the moment she wanted it. It was hard for him to relax. Instead of feeling his daughter kicking or squirming in Kayla's belly, his fingers drummed nervously on it. He itched to move. To open his laptop and work while whatever happened on TV happened. To have a drink and numb out to that scary hollowness trying to take him over, that hollowness that he worried was all that was left of his soul.

Early in the fall, as the leaves in Central Park began to change, he was in the conference room at seven thirty in

the evening. On the speaker phone was the lead buyer in the procurement department of Stanford University. How proud would his dad be if Patrick landed a deal to outfit all of Stanford's student centers and dorms with Airwaves? That could almost bring things full circle over the three generations of Armstrong men.

Kayla's face shone on his cell phone. That was the third time she'd called. Probably because he'd forgotten to tell her he'd be late again tonight. She should expect that by now. He let it go to voicemail as he continued his pitch to the buyer.

An hour later, the deal was struck. He and Nico went out to celebrate. So jubilant, he bought a round for the entire house, even though he didn't know anyone else at the bar. He was on top of the world again, a champion. Yes. His product would soon be in one of the most prestigious universities in the country. That would be amazingly good press. And that's the kind of thing that had legs, as the marketers said. When those students left the dorms, they'd miss their Airwave and would want to have one wherever they lived next.

Really, he should start contacting contractors of apartment complexes. Didn't they usually come with built-in microwaves?

His cell rang when he was on his second drink. His mother-in-law. Patrick downed his bourbon, slammed the glass back on the bar. This couldn't be good.

"Where are you?" she nearly screamed.

"I, uh," Patrick cowered over the bar, hoped she couldn't

hear the rowdy people behind him. "I just wrapped up an important meeting. What's up."

"Your daughter."

Twenty minutes later, Patrick ran into his wife's private room on the maternity floor at the hospital. Kayla, his beautiful, wise, kind, and loving Kayla, lay on the bed. Her damp curly hair splayed out over the pillow. In her arms, pressed tight to her bosom, was a newborn in a pink blanket—his daughter.

Getting to Kayla's bedside took an eternity. It felt like he was walking through wet cement during a slow time-warp. He saw only his wife's exhausted and lovely face, his daughter's tiny head. How had he missed this?

Kayla had called.

He had chosen not to answer.

He had chosen to not see his father's love his entire life and instead tried to replace that need with his work.

In the time since his father's death, he once again retreated into his work, and this time he chose not to see the beauty and love that was still in his life.

She looked up at him. The love in her eyes was quickly replaced with anger and sadness. Her brows pinched together. "Where were you?"

"I, um, there was a meeting . . ."

"Stop. I'm holding the most precious little girl on the planet. Do not destroy this moment with one of your lame excuses for missing your daughter's birth, Patrick," tears

streamed down her face. "Don't you love your family anymore? Love me?"

A deluge of tears burst out of him. How could he be so cruel? How could he not have seen what he was doing?

"Oh, Kayla." He collapsed on the bedside, tried to wrap his arms around his wife and newborn baby girl. "I'm so sorry. I'm so, so sorry. Please forgive me."

Chapter 10

"Y̶ou do realize this party is for kindergarten children, don't you?" Kayla followed him out of the bedroom and down the stairs of their new home in New Rochelle.

"Of course." Patrick straightened the throw pillows on the sofa on his way through the family room. In the kitchen, he poured a cup of coffee for both himself and Kayla. "Why do you ask?

They sat in the breakfast nook for their early morning one-to-ones as Patrick called it. On the day their sweet Ashley was born, the day Patrick realized how he was failing his wife by not being the support she needed when she needed it, he realized, too, how he was failing his children. He'd stepped into the restroom of Kayla's hospital room to wash his hands before holding his daughter for the first time and was shocked by what he saw in the mirror over the sink.

The puffy eyes, sallow skin, seahorse-like paunch hanging over his belt, and his unkempt hair, all signs he wasn't taking care of himself, signs he wasn't being the man he wanted to be for his family or his father. He'd made a commitment that day to clean himself up and run his

personal life as effectively and efficiently as his business. He owed most to his wife, his kids, and himself. "I will fully immerse myself into being the best, fittest version of me, no excuses, get it done." His pep talks to himself were legendary. He had snapped out of funks before. This was his new commitment to his family.

Now, just two years later, there he was trim and fit, thanks to his personal trainer. He and Kayla sipped coffee made by a Miele machine. They sat in the breakfast nook of the iconic mid-century mansion he owned. Well, not *quite* a mansion. Those weren't exactly abundant in that neck of the woods. He had the closest thing he could get, though. At just over 4,000 square feet, his professionally decorated and updated home was in the exclusive Isle of Sans Souci neighborhood. He didn't just have water views; their home was *on* the waterfront. His children would grow up in one of the wealthiest zip codes in the country and want for nothing.

"Seriously, Patrick. These kids are going to want cake, ice cream, and pizza. Not sushi."

"Nonsense." Patrick waved his hand in front of his face and realized that's what his father used to do. He smiled at Kayla's frowning face. "Well, we should at least have it on the side for the kids who do want sushi. Did I tell you I have a petting zoo coming?"

"Seriously? Patrick, we're renting a bounce house shaped like Thomas the Tank Engine and have face painters and balloon artists lined up. That's plenty. This party isn't lasting all day."

"Every kid wants to ride a pony and feed goats. They'll love it."

"Patrick—"

"Now about the food list for the parents—"

"Patrick." Kayla's voice had a tone that let him know she wasn't exactly thrilled with the conversation. "You have enough to do with work. Let me take care of the details of this party."

He stood, kissed her forehead, and returned to the kitchen. "I know you're more than capable. I just want this to be the best party my son could ever hope to have." He rinsed his coffee cup and placed it in the dishwasher after rearranging how the other glasses were lined up on the rack.

On the drive to the offices, which he'd moved to the Edge building right on Central Park West, where his company took up a full floor, he started his morning calls with his team. Raj, the CFO, and Nico both seemed to have that same almost-annoyed tone in their voices as Kayla did. What was wrong with this world? Yes, he could have let Raj handle the forecasts they were presenting to a venture capitalist firm. Sure, that was technically part of Raj's job description—making financial forecasts. Patrick just wanted to make sure it had his special touch on it. That VC company could give them what they needed to get their company to the next level: make it public. Man, Dad would be so proud.

At the office, his assistant Rhonda—no, that wasn't her name. Patrick nodded and smiled at her as he went

by. Renee. That was it. How could he forget that? Maybe because that position seemed to have a revolving door these days. He'd gone through how many now after Emily? Four? Five? Was that normal?

Renee came in as he unloaded his Italian leather attaché case. "Crazy thing." Her eyes squinted at him in annoyance and anger. "I called Marcum to place an order for promo products for the vendor show—"

"I fired his company." Patrick clicked into his email. "And you don't have to order them. I took care of that."

"Any reason why you couldn't tell me?"

Patrick straightened in his chair, slowly turned toward her. "Is that attitude necessary?"

Renee blinked at him. "Apparently." She turned around, took a few steps, then turned back to face him. "I already have my resignation letter written. Out of respect for the rest of the team, I'll try to stay on as long as it will take you to find a new assistant. Please don't dawdle."

And she was out.

Another one? Why was it this hard to find a loyal assistant? He paid well. He didn't have time to find another one. He punched Lorraine's extension on his phone and got her voice mail. As he left a message for his head of the People department to start looking for a new EA, he realized he hadn't spoken directly to Lorraine for a couple of weeks. Was she avoiding him? Why did it seem like his team wasn't the well-oiled machine it used to be? This company was a success. They were attracting VCs. He had plans to make an IPO one day. He couldn't have a

disgruntled force. He needed to change this culture.

He also needed to talk to Nico. Surely, he, Patrick, should be pitching that new luxury home goods company. No one knew this company better than he.

#

"Hold still, sweetheart." Patrick tried to wipe Ashley's face. Once again, she batted the cloth away with her small fingers. How could such tiny arms be that strong and fast?

"Maybe try letting her finish her dinner," Kayla suggested.

"Her dinner's all over her face. Why does she insist on eating with her hands." Patrick waited while Ashley smashed a fistful of penne pasta into her mouth, then tried to wipe off her cheeks again.

"Because she's two, Patrick. She hasn't mastered the fork yet."

Kayla must be tired today. He knew they should hire a nanny. Why had she been adamant she didn't want a live-in? "Do you think that's normal? She has good motor skills if you ask me."

"She's right on track, Patrick. Please, why don't you try enjoying your meal as much as she is?"

"The pennies are yummy, Daddy." Liam used his fork to rub his penne pasta into the garlic-butter sauce on his plate.

"It is son. I think you should eat more protein, though. Don't you like your chicken?"

"Patrick." Kayla put her fork down and stared at him. He held her eyes. "Yes?"

"When we're done here, it will be bath time, then we'll need to tuck these little ones in bed. Dinner is one of the few things we do together, can we please try to enjoy it?"

Patrick felt himself blink at her, then nodded. What did she expect from him? He was just trying to be helpful. And she knew he was trying to cut back on carbs. Why did she even make pasta tonight? The kids would be fine with chicken and brussels sprouts.

He kept his thoughts to himself. Things seemed to be slipping apart all over the place. The harder he tried to make sure everything was done the right way, the more things seemed to fall apart. How was this possible? He was successful. He was making big coin. They lived in one of the nicest houses in one of the most elite neighborhoods on the East Coast. His father would tell him where his family should be happy and where his team should be happy.

He never recalled his mother talking to his father with the same tone that Kayla used tonight. In fact, with the same tone she frequently used. When his father had passed away, there were tons of people who used to work for him who lauded him as a leader. Did they ever avoid him in the office? Did they sound annoyed when he spoke to them on the phone? And didn't Dad have the same assistant for, like, thirty years?

Patrick went to the gym to work out after dinner,

leaving Kayla alone to deal with bath and bedtime. He'd make up for it later in the week when he'd be able to get his workout in earlier in the day. She would understand. She always did.

Only that night, it appeared she didn't. He found her out on the deck, resting with a glass of white wine in her hand.

He took the chair beside her. "You should come to the gym with me. We could get a sitter . . ." He stopped in response to Kayla raising her hand, facing her palm toward him. Apparently, she didn't want to talk about going to the gym. "Are you okay?"

"Yes, and no." Kayla took a sip of her wine before looking directly at him. The deck lighting caught her green eyes, making flecks of gold appear. Those eyes still made him melt inside. "Yes, I'm fine. I'm healthy. I live in a safe and beautiful home. My children have everything they physically need and want."

"Life is perfect." Patrick nodded. "Why do you look so sad?"

"It's perfect for you, Patrick." She tilted her head toward him. "That doesn't mean it's perfect for the rest of us. I don't mean to sound ungrateful. Believe me, I appreciate the good income that affords us to be healthy and to live this well. Honestly, I'm grateful for it all. The thing is, Patrick." She paused and took a deep inhale. "It's all on your terms. I barely had any input in this house. Everything I do—correction, everything I attempt to do for this family, for me, for the kids, for you, is interrupted by you making

changes, or taking it over. I spent hours researching a piano teacher because *you* decided Liam should learn to play, and *you* ordered a piano, and *you* had it delivered without even asking me if I'd be available to accept the delivery. Then, because *you* hadn't thought my research was good enough, you hired a totally different teacher. And guess what? Liam has zero interest in it, nor is he really old enough to start lessons."

That was the tone she used when she sounded as if she were on the verge of tears.

"I don't understand why that upsets you, Kayla. I'm only trying to do what's best for our family. For you."

"What's best for our family is for you to be present with your children. What's best for me is for you to respect me. To remember that I do have a brain and can make decisions."

"I have no idea what you mean. I was present at the dinner table tonight, when *you* were trying to tell me how to parent."

"You were physically present, Patrick. Yes. You were not, however, present in the sense that you were aware of what your children were thinking, feeling, needing from you. And apparently, you're not able to be present with me like that right now either."

Kayla stood and went back into the house. Patrick almost followed her, then changed his mind. He'd let her cool off. It must have been a long day for her. Though doing what, he wasn't sure. He remembered, as treasurer of Liam's school's parent-faculty committee, she had a meeting with those drama-making mothers earlier in the day. He

remembered her mentioning that while she prepared that carb-laden dinner? He tried to be empathetic, though that was nearly impossible. Had she any idea how hard his work was? Had she forgotten how hard he worked?

At least she expressed some appreciation for the life he provided for her. Maybe he should plan another vacation. Granted, that European adventure he'd planned last summer hadn't gone off as well as he'd expected. Kayla was right about that one. Maybe the kids were too young for it. Still, it was a luxury trip all around. They stayed at the best hotels, had private guides, and the most amazing food. Did anyone say a thank you? He couldn't remember.

Nothing about this day seemed right. He seemed to be falling behind at home as much as at work, which just didn't make sense. They were doing well together as a family. His father would be proud to see how much he'd achieved. So, why wasn't he feeling any better about his life? Why did it seem no one else cared about it all as much as he did? Why can't everyone—Kayla, the kids, his team—why couldn't they understand he was working overtime to make things right for all of them?

He stood, stretched, felt a twinge in his back. His trainer had warned him about his form when he worked with the resistance bands. He'd forgotten about that tonight. Once more, he'd strained his back. An injury on yet another insult. Seemed about right—everything was backward.

What was he supposed to do? Work more? Try harder? He wasn't sure he had it in him.

Chapter 11

From the outside, it seemed every light in his house was turned on inside. All the windows glowed in the otherwise dark evening light. That was odd. Wasn't it past bedtime for the kids?

Patrick pulled into his garage. Oh . . . it was past bedtime. He was much later than he'd anticipated. Kayla must be having trouble getting them down. He should just find a nanny despite her objections. He knew eventually she'd be happy to have one.

He went through the mudroom and entered the kitchen. A couple of suitcases stood with their handles all the way up, as if waiting for someone to come along and pull them to their next destination. The titanium Tumi luggage set looked exactly like his family's. Checking the tag inside the leather holder confirmed it was. What was going on?

"Kayla." He headed into the main room. A basket of toys sat on the coffee table. "Kay?"

"Your dinner's in the warming drawer," Kayla entered the room with Ashley on her hip, and Liam tagging along behind her pulling a small suitcase of his own. "It's been in there since dinner. That was about four hours ago, and it may be too dried out to eat. I'm sure you'll be just fine fending for yourself."

"Fending?" Patrick was too stunned at the sight in front of him to know how to respond.

Kayla sat Ashley down on the sofa and squatted before the little girl to help her wiggle her cute feet into a pair of sandals.

"What . . . what's going on?"

"Are you really that blind?" Kayla stood and faced him. Her face was tear stained, eyes swollen.

"Are you upset because I was late for dinner?" Patrick reflected back on that night so many years ago with Erika. Her name hadn't entered his brain for a long, long time. He didn't like it being there now.

"No." Kayla wiped her face with her hands. "I'm upset because I finally realized what's been bothering me." She picked up the basket of toys from the table, brushed past him and went through the kitchen into the garage. Patrick followed behind.

"What did you realize?"

Kayla stopped by her SUV, then turned back toward him. "You've been lying to me for years."

Lying? Erika's note from long ago flashed through his mind.

"I don't understand." He tried, unsuccessfully, to block Kayla from opening the back of her SUV. "Don't I get an explanation? What have I lied to you about? I have always been faithful."

She placed the basket inside, and returned to the kitchen with Patrick on her heals. As if not hearing him, she grabbed the handles of luggage in the kitchen and returned

to the garage. Liam was behind them now, with Ashley bringing up the end of the line. He really didn't want to make a scene in front of the children. Yet, he couldn't just let them leave, could he?

Where were they going?

Kayla opened the rear passenger door of the SUV and helped Liam get in. He sat in his booster seat and clicked the seatbelt in. "Bye Daddy." He didn't even seem upset.

Kayla picked Ashley up. His sweet angel leaned out to give him her cheek as she often did—how many times had he come home after a long day of work just in time to kiss her cheek good night?

Kayla tucked her into her seat on the other side and connected the belt.

She closed the door and faced Patrick again. Tears were streaming down her face. "In case your curious, we'll be at my parents for the summer. At least for the summer."

"Curious? Of course, I want to know. I'm owed an explanation here, Kayla." Patrick tried to reach for her. She backed away.

"I need space Patrick. I need time and space to figure things out."

"Figure what out."

"Me. Us. Our family. I can't do this anymore."

"Do what."

"Live the role in the life you have scripted for me. There's no room for me to live how I want . . ." Her lower lip trembled as tears continued to spill down her face. "You've been lying to me for years, Patrick. Our relationship, our

family, our life together is all lived according to how you see things, how you want things. You say you love me."

"I do."

"You say you value me."

"I do." He heard the desperation in his voice as it rose an octave.

"No, you don't. You constantly disrespect my time, my energy. You don't value my ideas or my input. Everything is all about what you think is best. I can't take it anymore. I'd rather be a single mom, then stay in a pretend happy marriage."

With that she was gone.

He was alone in his house. His big, beautiful, perfect house.

How was this possible?

This was completely opposite of everything—he was a man of integrity, of values. He didn't operate in a way that hurt others.

Lying? Erika had blamed him for lying to her about his love for her. Maybe there was some truth to what she'd said. He'd never really given it much thought and now that he did, he wasn't as sure about whether he had truly loved her.

He knew he loved Kayla, though, and Liam and Ashley.

The lights were too bright in the house. He felt exposed; there was nowhere for him to hide. It was like being the suspect below the light bulb in an interrogation—only he was the one asking the questions as well as providing the answers.

How was it things came full circle as far as relationships

when everything was going right? He'd provided the perfect life for his family—yet it seemed as if he might have lost everyone.

All because he was late for dinner.

Again.

How many times had he been late?

Though that wasn't exactly what Kayla had said. The dinner was the last straw. What did she mean by "living the role he scripted for her"?

The night was long. Not only could he not sleep without her lying next to him, a collage of scenes from the past few years haunted him. How many times had that tone hit her voice when she'd remind him of what she'd taken care of when he wasn't there? It was the same tone his many assistants used until they left. The same tone that was now ever-present in Nico's voice. The same tone Raj had when he left his office earlier that day after Patrick told him he found a different insurer.

Was he going to lose them all?

Patrick almost didn't meet up with his golf buddies the next day. The idea of spending the day at home alone, however, was worse than showing up on the course looking and feeling the way he did. Kayla must have turned off her cell because she never answered all night nor the many calls that morning. He did get a call from his mother-in-law that let him know his wife and children were safe, and if he really cared for them, he'd leave them alone until they were ready for him.

They were ready for him? What about his feelings?

Those questions clawed at him on the drive to the golf club. He realized he was echoing Kayla's sentiments from last night. Had he really totally disregarded her throughout their marriage?

Had he only looked through his own, personal lens to view their lives? He only wanted the best for everyone. What was wrong with that lens?

Kayla wanted what was best for everyone, too. And she seemed to see things differently. Did she really think being separated from him was the best?

Maybe there was more than one definition of what was best.

#

"Patrick," Glenn's smiling face morphed into a look of concern when he spotted him. "Are you all right, man?"

Jay and Chris, who were putting things away in their lockers at the club turned to look at him, as well. They all seemed stunned.

"Yeah." Patrick guessed this meant his eyes were still bloodshot, and maybe he should have shaved that morning. He sat on a bench. "Well, actually, no. My wife left me last night."

He didn't expect an outpouring of support from his golf buddies. The four of them had played together for over a decade now. They never talked about anything in depth, always kept the chitchat to golf, business, and the occasional mention of a family. They weren't the kind of people he'd ever ask for help from.

He was wrong, though. These guys had his back.

Glenn sat next to him on the bench. "What happened?"

"I'm not sure I understand completely." Patrick related what had happened; repeated Kayla's parting lines. "Everything I've done since my father passed away has been for my family. I just wanted to set them up for the best, the easiest life possible."

"Did you ever ask them what they wanted?" Jay asked the question in a quiet voice, as if he wasn't sure he wanted the others to hear it.

Patrick met his eyes and shook his head.

"Yeah, man. Been there, done that." Jay smirked. "I don't know how it happened. My wife was a data scientist for a large bank when we met and married. She dealt with a ton of crazy stuff when she had a kid. When I found out, all of a sudden, I felt like I was the one who was supposed to be the big protector, the main provider, and without realizing it, I tried to take over and control our lives."

"How did you fix things?'

"Well, I didn't even notice it until the fighting escalated and she threatened to leave unless we got counseling."

"Wow." Patrick blew out a long breath. Maybe counseling could work for them.

"If you love your wife, listen to him Patrick." Chris pulled at his chin then showed him his hand. "Notice the wedding ring is gone?"

"Man, I'm sorry." How did he miss that? Where was he for his buddies? "I never knew."

"Well, I didn't exactly go around bragging that my wife left me."

Glenn patted him on the back and stood up. "The important thing is, you have time to fix it if you want to."

"How do I do that?"

"I think it begins by listening to your wife."

Patrick stood, approached his locker and opened it up. "The thing is, guys, as I thought about it last night, I think I'm pushing everyone away. Not just my family. The key people on my team. Everyone who's important to me, I'm driving them away. All I want is to lead us to—"

"You don't have to say any more." Glenn pulled his cell phone from his pocket. "I'm texting you the name of a guy, a life coach."

"You're kidding." Patrick kicked off his shoes, tossed them into his locker. "That's just what I don't need. To pay a guy a bunch of money to tell me how to set SMART goals and make a plan to get there." He pulled out his spiked golf shoes and returned to the bench. "I think setting goals and making a plan is what got me into this mess."

"This guy doesn't work like that. He takes for granted you already know how to be a success in business and teaches you how to be a success in life."

Success in life. That's what Patrick thought he was doing all along. Clearly, he needed help with it. Hopefully this guy could help him. "And you trust this guy? You're sure he knows what he's doing?"

Patrick watched as his friend texted the contact information to his phone.

"Dude," Glenn grinned. "I have his info in my phone because he's my life coach. I'd be splitting the proceeds

of my company with my ex-wife if it weren't for this guy helping me get my perspective right. Instead of winding up divorced, I wound up fixing my relationship with my wife, with my kids, and with my team at work. Yes, I'm sure 'this guy' knows what he's doing."

Patrick glanced at the text. The life coach was named Graham Norris, and he had a New York number. He promised himself he would call him first thing Monday morning. In the meantime, he'd pray all his relationships were still fixable.

Chapter 12

P atrick smiled and called "hello" to each member of his core team, all the C-suite personnel, the department leads, and his current assistant, Adelle, as they filed into the conference room. He received nods in return. There was no "How's it going?" aimed toward him, no attempt at camaraderie with him. Though judging by the ease and comfort they exhibited with each other—heads close together in whispered conversations, the occasional laugh—he realized they had bonded. Without him.

When everyone was seated, Adelle shut the door to the conference room, took her chair, and Patrick stood up.

"I'm sure you're all wondering what's going on, why I called this impromptu meeting." His eyes traveled the room, met Nico's, his most tenured personnel. He and Nico were tight at the beginning. Now, they barely spoke unless it was absolutely necessary. They hadn't sent texts about anything non-work related in years. Though Patrick remembered overhearing Nico joking in the breakroom about having to buy a round of drinks after hitting a hole-in-one at his club. Nico never mentioned such an amazing feat to Patrick. He hoped it wasn't too late to repair their relationship.

"Well, since today is Friday, my guess is this has to do with the all-hands meeting you called for Monday." Raj's voice was level, unemotional.

"You're right, Raj." Patrick smiled at him. "As you often are." Raj didn't smile back. He was another one who seldom spoke to Patrick. They'd had such a big blow up when it was time to renew insurance late last year that Patrick almost lost him then. Patrick had thought it a waste to continue with the interrupted-business part of the policy. Raj, always mild mannered, actually yelled, threatened to walk out and never come back until Patrick caved. Raj had been right back then. Just a few months later Patrick was astounded when there was a strike in France among truckers. Distribution ground to a halt in that country for two months. They sold nothing and had to give plenty of refunds. Thankfully, the lost revenue and expenses were covered by the insurance company. Only, Patrick realized now, he'd given in for the wrong reason. It was hard to find a replacement for Thad; he didn't want to lose Raj.

Thad. He needed to connect with him, too. Apologize and see how he could make amends.

"Are you selling the company?" Raj's question stirred up the room. Eyes opened wide. "Will there be mass layoffs next week?"

Everyone at the table started directly at Patrick.

"Is that it?" Nico asked. "If that's the case, I guess I don't have to hand you my resignation today. I mean, if someone else is taking over, maybe I'd like to be here for what's next."

"You're resigning?" Patrick pressed his hands on the conference table and leaned into them. Was he too late?

"A lot of us are just waiting for the next opportunity." Jacqueline, a department lead piped in. She glanced nervously around the room. Many nodded at her.

"I'm one of them." Taylor lifted his chin. "I've been your head of procurement for over five years, and I want to actually do my job. I want to work at a place where the boss will not constantly override my decisions or make deals without consulting me or that they think are not in the best interest of the company."

"I get it. I really do." Patrick nodded as he stood straight and tall. "And I hope I can convince each of you to stay." He cleared his throat. "Without going into all the details as to why, I've been seeing . . . well, I've been getting some guidance on how I'm handling my life as well as my business."

Nico leaned back in his chair, crossed his arms over his chest, and raised his eyebrows at Patrick.

"Are you selling the company?" Raj's question stirred up the room. Eyes opened wide. "Will there be mass layoffs next week?"

"No."Patrick continued, "I realized that I haven't been the great leader I always wanted to be. In fact, I wasn't really leading. I was doing everyone else's jobs."

Nico smirked.

"And that's created a little friction among us," Patrick continued. "Well, a lot of friction between all of you and me. I see it now. I really do. Please know, that isn't the way

I envisioned the culture of this company. I don't know why I did it—actually I do. Honestly, I never doubted anyone's abilities. I just had my vision of how things were supposed to go; it never occurred to me there would be other visions, maybe even better ones."

He paused as he took his chair at the board table. He cleared his throat before speaking. "I called you in to tell you that, going forward, there will be major changes around here. Changes that I need you to help me define and implement. I don't want to lead this company by myself. I want—I need your input, your feedback, your expertise—because I finally realize the lens I use to see the universe is just that: a lens. And there are others that maybe can see from a different perspective that will lead to better outcomes."

Nico's smirk turned into a genuine smile. He nodded at Patrick.

"For those of you willing to stay with me, I'd like to talk about how we can restructure the company, give people more responsibilities, open up new opportunities. Who's in?"

#

Despite how well things went with the team, Patrick still had reservations about entering into his in-laws' house as he drove to their place out in Oyster Bay on Long Island. He'd been making the hour-long drive on Saturdays to spend time with his children over the past couple of weeks. This time, he asked Kayla if he could come over on Friday evening, just to speak with her. She'd refused to meet him anywhere except her parents' house, where he knew the watchful eye of his mother-in-law would not be far away. She had yet to forgive Patrick for not arriving at the hospital in time there for Ashley's birth. The brief exchanges he'd had with her when he picked up or dropped off the kids on Saturdays indicated forgiveness might never come from her.

Regardless, he couldn't lose his family.

Cynthia was outside, watering her potted plants on the front porch when he arrived. He knew his in-laws had a housekeeper who came three days a week to maintain the property, which included watering the plants. His mother-in-law must have learned he was coming and was waiting to speak to him before he entered the house.

"Hello, Patrick." She stood at the front of her porch, on the top of three steps, looking down at him.

"Hello, Cynthia. How are you?"

"I am well." She pointed the spout of the watering can toward him. "When are you going to fix things? You've been coming here every Saturday and spending time with the kids. This isn't fair to anyone. Thankfully, Ashley is really too young to understand what's going on. Poor Liam, though, is confused. Indecision on the part of parents is never a good thing, Patrick."

"I'm not undecided about anything. I want my family back. I want to make things right with Kayla and the kids." The rest of his words were a bit harder to get out. "And to make right with you and John. I know it can't feel good to . . . to watch your daughter feel so . . . so hurt."

Cynthia raised an eyebrow. "Patrick, I've never seen you exhibit any kind of empathy. It gives me hope."

He shrugged. "Well, I'm sincere."

"Good. Now what?"

"Really, I was hoping Kayla and I could go away for the weekend and talk. Both of us talk and actually listen to each other." He rubbed his forehead, ran his hand through his hair. "She wouldn't even meet me out at a restaurant tonight. I can't imagine a weekend at a place of her choice is out of the question."

"Her choice?" The corners of Cynthia's mouth turned down. "Hmm. Give me a few minutes with her. Take a seat here on the porch."

He did as told and waited—eternally optimistic—he imagined his mother-in-law talking Kayla into going away with him. He couldn't figure out why she would do that, and it didn't matter. Cynthia was a force to be reckoned with. If anyone could talk Kayla into doing this, it was her mother.

Sure enough, about fifteen minutes later, when thoughts started seeping into Patrick's head that perhaps Cynthia was playing a trick on him and abandoning him on the porch, the door opened. His beautiful, green-eyed Kayla came out, wheeling an overnight bag.

He ran the few steps to her and stopped. She turned sideways and held her hand up to let him know not to get too close.

"I'm not doing this because I'm happy to see you, Patrick. I'm doing this because Liam is confused. Because

Ashley isn't quite sure who you are anymore." She blinked at him. "And because, frankly I'm confused too, and I don't know who you are anymore."

"Oh, Kayla. I'm sorry. I really am. And I appreciate this opportunity to connect with you." He held his arm out, pointing toward his car. "Where would you like to go?"

Kayla tilted her head, jutted out her chin. "East."

"Is that the name of a place?" He wasn't all that familiar with Long Island and wasn't sure if he'd ever remembered hearing of a town called East.

"No, Patrick." Kayla stepped off her parents' porch and dragged her bag on the flagstone walk toward the driveway. "It's a direction," she cast a glance over her shoulder.

He ran to catch up with her and opened the back of his car. "I don't understand."

Kayla let him take her bag and place it in the trunk next to the spare bag he always had in case he wanted an extra change of clothes after a round of golf. He shut the trunk and saw her standing, hands on hips, as if she expected a challenge.

"I want to head east on the island. Just drive until we see a town or place that looks nice, then find a Bed and Breakfast or a nice place to stay for the weekend."

Yes, this was a challenge. Patrick never did anything that impulsive. He planned, he strategized, he made sure all the details were just right. How else could anyone expect to be at a place they'd like? Or have the best time possible? The old Patrick would have argued. No. The old Patrick would have already had a place lined up for them.

Kayla didn't realize she wasn't talking to the old Patrick. She was talking to the one terrified of disappointing her and the children.

"Sounds like a great adventure." He clapped his hands. "You lead the way."

# # #

Two hours later, Patrick and Kayla checked into a place called the Ram's Head Inn out on Shelter Island. It was only rated two-stars and Patrick knew nothing about Shelter Island—other than it wasn't part of the Hamptons. The building was over a century old and was decorated accordingly with authentic antiques of an age and era Patrick knew nothing about.

Kayla was delighted with it all. They checked in, found their room, then went down to the restaurant, where they chose a table outside on the patio. The heat of the warm summer evening was kept in check by a soft breeze. The view was simply magnificent—the resort sat up on a rise. They could look over the manicured property down to the beach, to the water below. This was amazing. How could he not know this place existed? Oh, because he'd always insisted on staying at the Hamptons when he took the family for long weekends on Long Island. He'd been closed off to other ideas. The Hamptons were supposed to be the best.

He turned to Kayla. "Are you ready to talk now?"

She gave him a soft smile. He had agreed not to talk during the drive, telling him she wanted to enjoy the scenery and give herself a chance to figure out exactly what

she wanted to say. She asked him if he'd have the grace to grant her that opportunity.

Grace. She'd said "grace." The idea that his wife, his beloved wife, had to ask him to have the grace to allow her to think nearly made him cry. What kind of egomaniac monster had he been?

"Yes." She sipped her white wine. "I think I'm ready. Only I'd like you to go first. I'm curious why now you're willing to just drive East until we find a place that looks nice."

"I guess you could say I finally realized I don't have all the answers."

Kayla giggled. "Honestly, Patrick, I always admired your confidence. One of the things I love about you is that when you know what you want, you see no obstacles in the way of getting it. Though I had no idea you thought you had all the answers."

"I didn't know I thought that way, either." Patrick stretched his hand over the table, placed it palm up. "I did know that I wanted to give you and the kids the best life possible. I worked a lot to ensure we had the money to do whatever we wanted . . . correction, to do whatever I wanted my family to experience."

She placed her hand on his.

"I don't know how that all got twisted around. I mean, it seems I spent my entire life misunderstanding what real happiness was all about."

"What do you mean?"

"When I first started the company, I thought if I reached

the level of success my parents did, then they'd be proud of me, and I'd feel good about myself. That led to me being estranged from them for way too long, because I felt like I could never live up to their expectations of success, money, achievement, whatever. In truth, all they wanted was for me to be happy, to have a solid and secure life, and be happy."

She squeezed his fingers.

"When Dad died, and I realized much to late what he wanted for me, something in me kind of broke. You remember those days—all the booze, the constant work—just to avoid feeling that pain, that grief over missing out on my father."

"I do remember. And honestly, Patrick, I understood." She tilted her head toward him. "I knew you were grieving your father. That's why I forgave you when you were late to Ashley's birth. And you changed then."

"Right. I didn't want to have what happened with my dad and me to happen with you and me. That's when things got all twisted. I became laser focused on doing what I thought I was supposed to do, as if there was only one right way to do things. Patrick briefly closed his eyes, feeling the pressure of tears build up. "I'm deeply sorry, Kayla. I wish I could undo all the bad parts of the past couple of years. I can't. I can try to make up to you for the next couple years—no, the rest of our lives together."

He met her eyes. They, too, glistened with tears. "What would that look like, Patrick? How will things be different?"

He sniffed. "For one thing, I'll work less."

Kayla removed her hand, leaned back in her chair and crossed her arms. "By what magic?"

"Well, I ended the day at the office today with everyone on my core team. If you think I've been a control freak at home, you should have seen me at the office."

"I've heard."

Of course she had. She was friends with Nico's and Raj's wives. The three couples used to do things together. Raj had a daughter the same age as Liam. They probably still had play-dates together, and Patrick had been too busy to notice. He would fix that, too.

"Well, I spent the afternoon with the core team apologizing and getting their input on how to lead the company from here out. Things will be different. I will be home every night for dinner. I will be there for you and the kids."

"Your physical presence isn't enough." Kayla dropped the defensive position, though she placed her hands in her lap instead of returning one back in Patrick's still on the table.

"I understand that, too." He took a sip of his Cabernet. "That will be different, too. I'll need your help with that, though. Old habits might creep back in from time to time. Please know you need to call me out on it. I will do my best to be the man I used to be—the one who listened to you— who was your partner not your manager."

Kayla's smile returned to her face. "I'll call you out on it. I will."

A flutter of hope filled his heart. "Does this mean you'll come back to me?"

"This means I'll come back to you." She squeezed his fingers. "Liam will be so happy. Ashley will, too."

"Do you think they'd like this place? It's absolutely gorgeous. Maybe we could go get them tomorrow and bring them back here."

"I think they'd prefer Sesame Place."

"Where?"

"The water park in the Poconos."

"I've never heard of it."

Kayla smirked.

Patrick recognized what he'd just done. "Though if you think that's where they'd like to go, let's take them."

Epilogue

Here are the next steps to take your mental game to the next level and live the life of your dreams:

1. Go to www.eternaloptimistpodcast.com and check for the newest learning updates, visit our retail store for logoed merchandise, and experience our library of the podcast and the books I've read

2. Subscribe, Rate, and Review The Eternal Optimist Podcast on all major podcast platforms

3. Follow The Eternal Optimist Podcast on Instagram and Facebook

4. Follow The Eternal Optimist Channel on YouTube

5. Connect with me, author Matt Drinkhahn, on LinkedIn

You control your destiny from this moment forward.

If that were true, what conditions would need to be present? You and I don't control if a natural disaster occurs on the other side of the world, and we don't control who our parents are or where we live at birth. We don't control the US economy or if the driver will really deliver that package "Next-Day" without damage. We have zero control over many of the variables in this world and sometimes we have a great degree of control. Only two certainties exist for anyone reading this book; you control your attitude and your effort.

Before we go any further and set up the chessboard, let's be clear that this is NOT a book of eternal optimism where everything is "Pollyanna", where all the evil in the world can be turned to the good, where all challenges can be overcome by simply "smiling your way through them". That's not true optimism, it's naivete at best and close-minded blindness at worst.

What is eternal optimism? To quote my guest Rocky Garza from The Eternal Optimist Podcast: "Eternal optimism is a mindset of looking at the world through a lens that sees further down the road than what lays directly at one's feet right now, rather always seeing that good can be found from what is happening now."

We can change. We can overcome. We can do whatever we put our minds to, period. We simply need to learn how to do this in the areas of our lives that matter. Hence begins the game!

Welcome to Life: the game.

Life is like traveling around a big circle that goes round and round, repeatedly. Imagine a 365-day year as one revolution around the circle.

The variables in this game are endless! And they are constantly evolving and influencing how we play the game.

What do we actually control in this game? There are mini games like parenting, business, and love, to name three. Every relationship could be a game, with everyone having an endless number of moves in that game alone. Are you playing checkers or chess? Or perhaps Othello or Backgammon? What does winning the game mean to you? Might it mean reaping a reward? Or getting recognized as someone of significance? Or escaping out of a living hell crowded on all sides by misery and injustice? Or simply "being"? Or living a life virtuously according to your spiritual beliefs? Ask 100 people what it means to win in the game of life, and you'll get 100 different answers. So many lenses one might look through in how to play the game...

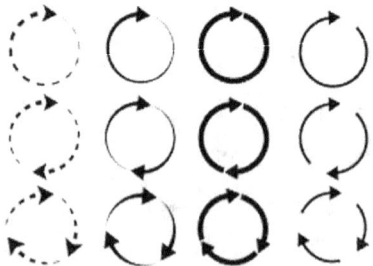

Try on lenses in such categories as our senses, money, parents, environment, and nutrition. There are social variables present in the time in which we live. These include the shifting (or stagnant) winds of politics, religion, long-held family beliefs, cultural norms, peer pressure, our own awakening, etc. And some people are playing a game to thrive in business and life, while many more may not see life as a game at all. They may see it a struggle to survive the day.

Additionally, there are geographical variables in play. A person living in New York City will experience the world differently than someone living in Charlotte, NC or Seattle, Washington. And consider that 95% of the world population is living outside of the United States and their worldviews are shaped by a different narrative. If you're American, Australian, British, Canadian, Danish, Dominican, Indian, Iraqi, Mexican, Nigerian, Pakistani, Vietnamese, Zimbabwean, or anywhere in between, we all play the game of life and we all might do it differently.

Let's remember to layer into the game that we are emotional beings with fear, anger, joy and sadness baked into the cake. Some psychologists expand this list to include four more emotions like trust, surprise, disgust, and anticipation. Wherever one stands on the emotional platform, we can agree that emotions are felt, they influence the game differently at different times, and they are constantly shifting.

There are some constants that do not shift for us in such obvious ways. One constant to the best of the public knowledge, is that TIME passes at the same rate for each of us. This book isn't about debating beliefs on that topic, it's about YOUR EXPERIENCE OF LIFE and WHAT YOU CONTROL.

And these two things, Attitude and Effort, are the only two things we truly ever control. And in this Game of Life, attitude and effort matter. Where is your blind spot with your attitude and effort? With so many places to search, we're sure to uncover many opportunities to improve our attitude and effort, we simply need look for them and know how to unlock their potential.

With all the possible advantages and disadvantages that one might be born with or grow up to realize, we must

move forward with them right now. Someone once said that it is up to us to learn to "play the hand we're dealt". Whether it's exciting or dull, hopeful or full of despair, simple or perilously difficult, silver spoon-born or from the dregs of poverty, it's a journey of both body and mind and we all play it. HOW we play it, with our attitude and effort, is up to us.

And one can control their attitude and their effort starting right NOW.

When Victor Frankl wrote his timeless classic *Man's Search for Meaning*, chronicling the horrors he experienced while imprisoned in a Nazi concentration camp during World War II in Europe, he was challenged in both his attitude and his effort. Read that book and observe all the variables that went into his experience. The most gruesome, unthinkable things happened in front of him, to him, around him, every day for years—and his perspective was still one of hope. His attitude endured. His effort was forced to do things he would've otherwise not have chosen to do, and he still controlled it. If he can endure that experience and come out the other side inspiring us all that we can do it, then there's hope for us too.

Frankl's attitude was trained on keeping his "freedom" in his mind so that the enemy had no mental dominion over him. They may have had his body and forced his actions, yet they couldn't break his will spirit or will to live. That's how important one's attitude is.

I wrote this book to illustrate for everyone who will take note, that we may or may not have control over all our circumstances AND we always have the power to control our response to them. The opportunity rests within us. What we "know" at the ages of 23 or 46 or 69 might be different than what we "knew" years before it. This book chronicles the journey of our main character through several important "defining moments" in his life and those around him. *How he responded in his early years is far different than how he responded as he aged and learned. There is always the chance to change our minds.*

> **"Progress is impossible without change, and those who cannot change their minds cannot change anything."**
>
> **— George Bernard Shaw**

How might we learn to change our minds? To learn, adapt, and grow as we take in new experiences in our lives? Curiosity of "why" is paramount to this quest in owning one's mindset. One thing you'll take away from this book is a list of questions to challenge you to think.

- Why does this frustrate or anger me?
- Why do I feel "down" right now?
- Why does that person with no means and seemingly little resources appear to be happy while I am miserable or depressed?
- Why does my significant other keep saying to me "that you might hear me but you're not listening?"

- What is it about me that I can OWN in this situation so I might show up and learn from these challenges I'm presented with now?

- How might I learn from this person who is spewing negativity or hate so that I might understand where they're coming from?

- How might I do the best with what I have right now?

When we're curious, we have the gift of learning at our fingertips. Let's lean into it together on this journey.

"You play the hand you're dealt. I think the game's worthwhile."
— Christopher Reeve

Christopher Reeve, the original Superman (at least to me he was, I'm an 80's kid) said these words after he suffered a horrific fall from a horse during a 1995 equestrian competition causing irreparable spinal cord damage leaving him paralyzed at the age of 42. He needed a ventilator to breath and constant care for the rest of his life. His wife Dana's life also pivoted at that moment into one of being a constant caregiver to her husband. His pursuit of acting success changed into one of advocacy and research for such injuries.

"Play the hand you're dealt."

These words were also spoken by Jawaharlal Nehru, a central figure in India's move to independence from the British Raj in 20th century. He was tapped by Mahatma Gandhi to be his political heir and after being imprisoned

wrongfully for a long sentence, he became India's first Prime Minister in 1947 upon India's independence.

And the stories could continue on the roller coaster of defeat to victory, back and forth, for ALL of us. We all have our story. No matter where yours has come from or where it is now, you can craft your own story starting NOW. You simply need to commit to the process of learning how to change and be steadfast along the way.

"When we are no longer able to change a situation - we are challenged to change ourselves."

— Viktor Frankl

Everyone lives two lives, one in public and one in their own mind. It is in this collision of the two worlds in every person on earth that all variables and conditions intersect first. In this juncture between our inner world and the world around us, we begin this book in our search for meaning and fulfillment.

For anyone who made it this far, I commend you for your curiosity and thirst for learning. The thirst is real and when curiosity is a core value, the thirst is unquenchable. AND we love that!

Continue this journey with me and together we'll keep growing and impacting the world in a positive way together.

Here are the lessons we'll discover together:

- How to overcome your greatest fears
- How to show up at peace when others judge us

- How to live "on purpose and in alignment" with your mission
- How to reflect and learn each month so that every year allows breakthroughs
- How to ask questions that empower (as we leave scarcity mindset in our wake!)
- How to become comfortable with your emotions
- How to let go of and accept our "stuff" so that it has no more weight over us
- How to make tiny tweaks in one's daily life that will uplift one to live the life of their dreams!
- How to develop and strengthen a rock-solid culture throughout your family and business
- How to grow and strengthen all business and personal relationships
- How to ask for what you want and have a great chance at getting it!
- How to strategize, plan, and execute on your goals and dreams!

We can work on these things together one-on-one or as part of our Eternal Optimist Podcast community.

Here are the next steps to take your mental game to the next level and live the life of your dreams:

6. Go to www.eternaloptimistpodcast.com and check for the newest learning updates, visit our retail store for logoed merchandise, and experience our library of the podcast and the books I've read
7. Subscribe, rate, and review The Eternal Optimist

Podcast on all major podcast platforms

8. Follow The Eternal Optimist Podcast on Instagram and Facebook

9. Follow The Eternal Optimist Channel on YouTube

10. Connect with me, author Matt Drinkhahn, on LinkedIn

> Wherever you are, you're at the wheel.
> You're the driver.
> Let's get there together.
> Stick with it, you can do it my friend.
> Matt Drinkhahn

About Matt Drinkhahn

"My Mission is to push people to be the best they can be and to OWN that we were all made with limitless potential."

Matt is an accomplished entrepreneur and sales expert, driven by his love for his family and his passion for helping others believe in themselves. With a career sales total of over $130 Million, he has made a name for himself as a coach and speaker, working with renowned organizations such as Equitable, Vector Marketing, Red Hat, CoreNet, Tarkett, and more.

In 2015, Matt faced a life-altering zip line accident that left him unable to walk and in constant pain. However, he turned this adversity into an opportunity for growth, coaching, and inspiring others while lying flat on his back. His determination and positive mindset led to his best year in business in 2016, a testament to the power of eternal optimism.

Since 2014, Matt has been coaching recovering perfectionists to grow themselves and their companies. Matt has facilitated numerous retreats and conferences while providing one-on-one and team coaching.

Matt is a member of the Front Row Dad community of family men with businesses. He resides in Charlotte, NC, with his amazing wife Julie and their three daughters. Tune into The Eternal Optimist Podcast, where Matt shares his insights and experiences with the aim of inspiring others to embrace their limitless potential and strive for greatness.

Check out his life's work on the social media channel of your choice below:

And be sure to check out Matt's LIVESTREAM Monday through Friday at 7:00am ET on the Facebook and Instagram Eternal Optimist Podcast accounts below!

Website:
- eternaloptimistpodcast.com

Instagram: Eternal Optimist Podcast
- instagram.com eternaloptimistpodcast/

Facebook: Eternal Optimist Podcast
- facebook.com/eternaloptimistpodcast

LinkedIn:
- linkedin.com/in/mattdrinkhahn/

YouTube: Eternal Optimist Podcast
- youtube.com/@eternaloptimistpodcast8000

Twitter: @MDrinkhahn
- twitter.com/MDrinkhahn

"Working Together to Achieve YOUR Goals and Dreams."

More Testimonials

"During a season of unpredictability in my life, I was seeking counsel and perspective from anyone with wisdom to share. Matt Drinkhahn answered that call with time, insight, and a genuine sense of curiosity and empathy. I felt truly seen and served by a stranger who quickly became a brother. It's rare to find such authentic human connection, and I'm beyond grateful for the support and optimism Matt brought when I needed it the most."

— **Mike Abramowitz**, Partner with Better Than Rich; Front Row Dad

"I can count on one hand the people that have had a positive impact on me the way Matt has. He's unique in many ways. His energy, his experience, his perspective, did I mention his energy? His knowledge. He's an amazing dad and husband to his children and wife. He's an amazing friend and mentor to all that create space for him to exist in their worlds. The world is better with Matt in it, I know my world is."

— **Josh Goodman**, Founder & CEO

"A few times in your life you meet someone that changes your life dramatically for the better. Matt was one of those times. Matt taught me a way to structure my sales strategy which dramatically increased my already successful sales career, inspired me to start my own business, and most importantly put my wife and two kids first in life. I will always be thankful for Coach Matt."

– **Frank Wiseman**, Global Account Executive at Tarkett

"Patience and grace. These are two things I appreciate about Matt Drinkhahn's intentions to be an amazing friend, human, and *Eternal Optimist*. In working with Matt, I've practiced being patient with myself and others, and I've given more grace to myself and others. In so doing I have become more optimistic about my future, the future of my business, and my relationships with my family, the people I work with and the world in general. Let's go bubba."

– **Phil Bohlender**, Vector Marketing; Front Row Dad

"I've gotten to know Matt Drinkhahn really well over the last few years. I know his story, his family, his strengths, his challenges, and all the beautiful things that make him highly unique. I've watched him grow and serve people in amazing ways. One of Matt's gifts is his ability to see light in dark places. He navigates life with an authentic aura that makes people smile. He responds to adversity with strength and compassion. He brings positive energy to everything he touches. Matt is a powerful beacon of light shining optimism into the world. That's what makes him an impactful leader. That's how he elevates humanity. That's why I feel grateful and privileged to experience life with him. "

— **Ali Jafarian**, Founder, Community Builder; Front Row Dad; Podcast Host of SPACE

"Matt Drinkhahn possesses an incredibly positive attitude, an enthusiasm for his family, friends, and the people he works with, and an absolute love of life that will rub off on anyone with whom he comes into contact. His ability to connect with people and guide them towards recognizing and surmounting their

challenges is unparalleled. Matt's expertise in this field makes him an invaluable source of wisdom and inspiration for anyone seeking to enrich their lives."

— **Matt Sprang**, Facilitator and Small Business Owner

"I know Matt to be an incredible father, husband, coach, and friend. And while the list of attributes that contribute to his awesomeness is nearly endless, it is his persistent curiosity, unending optimism, and fervent willingness to learn from both his successes and his missteps that underpin his incredible success."

— **Michael W. Wagner** – Storage Rebellion; Front Row Dad

"It is very rare to have a relationship start on a pledge to be nothing but honest and unwavering in making each other truly better and even more rare to be consistent in that pledge over a considerable length of time. Matt has honored his word and surpassed my expectations as a coach, colleague, and friend. I am a better man because of our time together."

— **Dr. Thomas Schmolze**, EdD, Rock Hill Schools Superintendent

"My world and my team's world have been greatly improved by the personal and professional input from Matt. Matt brings a systemic approach to tackling problems where I previously used "my gut feeling" to maneuver. My ability to elevate others and ensure people are in the best places for their own success has grown since employing his "brain shark" strategies. Not only has he helped me double my business in the short time we have worked together, but more importantly he has helped me ensure my business is supporting my personal and family goals as well.

If you have the good fortune of learning from this guy, run with the opportunity."

— **Blair Martin**, Managing Principal

"When I come across an author/speaker/coach that I feel I have instant alignment with, I lean in to everything they do. Matt Drinkhahn is that kind of person. Matt has decided to live his life with absolute intention, and yet leaves himself opportunities for spontaneity and abundant time with Team Drinkhahn (his wife and girls). I've seen the impact of Matt's rare ability to listen to others. And Matt's optimistic, yet tactical approach at business and life should be something every family man with a business absorbs and implements."

— **Kyle Reedstrom**, Founder of Passive 25K Group

"I just wanted to take a moment to express admiration for my friend, Matt Drinkhahn. Matt navigates life with an abundance of energy, an ever-present smile, and an unwaveringly positive attitude. His optimistic outlook is as impressive as it is contagious! I consider every interaction with Matt not only time well spent, but even more, a blessing."

— **Paul Gollnick**, VP of Sales; Real Estate Investor; Follower of Christ; Front Row Dad

"Life is short. You want to spend time with those that lift your spirits and add value to you. Matt's optimism, sense of humor, and genuine nature is infectious. He's curious and eager to dig deep to find how he can have an impact on you. I'm always better after spending time with Matt."

— **Ray Bayat**, Front Row Dad

"I've known Matt for a couple of years, and can say with absolute sincerity that I've never seen him without a smile on his face. More importantly, it's rare to engage with Matt and not end up smiling yourself. He's kind of fun, genuine, warm, and always very curious. I'm a big fan of him and the things that he does and can't wait to see the impact his book on the world."

— **Kasim Aslam**, Founder of Solutions 8; Co-Host of Perpetual Traffic Podcast

"When I think of positivity, optimism, and resilience, I think of Matt Drinkhahn. We've laughed, celebrated, cried, and learned together over the past couple years and I can sincerely share that he's authentic and a real positive influence. He's always looking for the lessons in the moment and constantly curious as to how to show up for others."

— **Grant Baldwin**, Founder & CEO at The Speaker Lab

"Matt Drinkhahn, aptly known as 'The Eternal Optimist', embodies a refreshing perspective on life. His mantra, 'With gratitude in your heart, it's impossible not to be an optimist', truly reflects his unwavering positivity. Beyond his optimistic outlook, Matt's ability to listen attentively and engage with thoughtful questions makes interactions with him both enlightening and uplifting."

— **Jason Hylan**, CEO

"Matt has one thing at the front of his mind at all times, and that's seeing the good in everything. He is curious, he is kind, and, without fail, every interaction I've had with him leads me to not only see the world through a different lens but see myself in a way that

I hadn't before. He is the teacher of good lessons and at his core a good man."

— **Rocky Garza** - Speaker/Coach to Purpose Driven Companies

"Simply brilliant story telling. Matt is an inspirational force. Simple and easy are not the same thing and I can't thank Matt enough for putting it that way. I love how much I'm learning from life now that I'm viewing challenges as opportunities. Thank you, Matt, for helping me to live a value centered life and be a better me! I am your Bob, and you are my Dr. Marvin and I'm proud to say that thanks to you I'm taking baby steps towards being a better me, every day and every moment in every aspect of my life."

— **Tom Schneller**, Emmy Award-winning Broadcast Engineer

"Matt Drinkhahn continues to personally and professionally inspire and challenge my views on optimism through his consistent pursuit of it. He shows up in raw honesty, always looking for the lesson that optimism might bring to the table. Matt is both the friend and colleague that I call upon when I need insight, clear language, alternative perspectives, and practical next steps. He doesn't just slap a 'positive spin' on things but embodies genuine optimism through his careful selection of word, thought and action."

— **Alicia Byers**, Strategist and Coach for The Financial Advisor; ProAdvisor Coach

"A competitive young adult turned into a fiercely passionate, reflective, and awake husband and father. I am lucky to know

Matt and he has made a huge impact on my life and career. When I think of Matt, I think of progress. I have always known Matt to be competitive and perform highly in wherever he immerses himself, and if there is a way to win or if someone is keeping score, watch out!"

— **Josh Greco**, Host of ProAdvisor Coach Podcast, Master Coach – ProAdvisor Coach

"Working with Matt has really helped me as the visionary and CEO of our firm think about areas of the business that I normally would not have thought of. He brings such a unique perspective to our meetings, and I always come away with something I was not even thinking about. When you do that each week and add the compounding impact of those decisions over a few years this has significantly changed the trajectory of our firm for the positive."

— **Dillan Micus**, CEO & Owner

"Matt has been a positive and driving influence in my career. He has steered me in a direction that I could have never done alone. He knows how to get the most out of you but also knows the right drivers to build one's practice for optimal growth and success."

— **Evan Press**, Leader and Entrepreneur

"When a business relationship evolves into a friendship, that's a hallmark of something meaningful. Matt has played a big role in my professional life over the past few years, and I'm proud to call him a friend as well. Maintaining a positive mindset can be a true test of endurance, and Matt has been a guiding light for me with each challenge I've thrown his way."

— **Phil Kim**, Founding Member and Managing Director

"I had the pleasure of meeting Matt at a Front Row Dads' retreat, where we bonded over our shared commitment to being great fathers and husbands. He's the voice behind *The Eternal Optimist* podcast, a title that perfectly encapsulates his outlook on life. In every interaction, his positivity is infectious, yet what truly sets him apart is his introspective nature. He's not afraid to delve deep, question himself, and adapt his views as he grows, making him a genuinely inspiring figure in my life."

— **Kendall Kirk**, Front Row Dad

"As the adage goes, 'you are the sum of the five people you surround yourself with.' Make sure one of those people is Matt Drinkhahn. Without a doubt, Matt is one of the most insightful people out there with a helluva ability to truly read, understand, and connect with people. There are a lot of people in my world who deal with facts, data, insights, graphs, and anecdotes. In a world awash with disparate data, the rare gems are when you find something or someone who offers wisdom instead. Matt's personal and professional accomplishments speak to how he has accumulated so much data and anecdotal knowledge; nevertheless, it is because of his unique ability to listen and truly connect with people, both professionally and personally, that makes every interaction with him an enjoyable learning experience. Despite all these strengths, his true superpower is his ability to find eternal optimism in this day and age when it is so easy to be cynical. When you know Matt, you get wisdom paired with his unending optimistic support which is a potent mix for anyone trying to be the doer of great deeds—whether they be professional or personal. I'm not sure if it was recommended to compartmentalize and have a professional group of five people, and a personal

group of five people with which to surround yourself, but if they are supposed to be separate circles, make sure Matt is in both."

— **RJ Caster**, CEO of Techne

"Matt has been a friend and mentor for almost a decade. He always inspires with contagious encouragement, clear focus, and most importantly, with a kind approach. He is truly the eternal optimist!"

— **Wendy Baum**, Partner at Infinity Strategic Partners, LLC

"There is no better way to describe 'Coach Matt' than to say he is the embodiment of 'The Eternal Optimist'. His positive energy radiates. It's undeniably infectious. If you're ready to 'take out the head trash' and redefine success, Matt will be your accountability partner."

— **W. Sandy Solomon**, Covenant Advisory Group, Charlotte NC.

"Drinkhahn is not only my business coach, but also my mentor and friend. His attitude has helped me to surpass my way of thinking. I have not had the opportunity to read the book before it comes out, but whatever he's written, I can guarantee it will be INCREDIBLE."

– **Ken Mika**, CEO of Politicoin

"What first struck me about Coach Matt is his amazing energy and enthusiasm. I've yet to have the pleasure of meeting him in person, but we've spent countless hours on Zoom together and he makes you feel every time like he's right there in the room with you. Then, he hits you with a thoughtful comment and you're just

blown away by the combination of presence and wisdom."

— **Mitch Nachtigall**, Entrepreneur; Front Row Dad

"Matt Drinkhahn brings a positive, uplifting, and inspiring energy to all that he does. He has helped me step out of my comfort zone and grow as a professional. It has been a great pleasure getting to know him both on a professional and personal level. Wishing you continued success and blessings on this new adventure Matt."

— **Patti Dziedzic**, Office Manager and Leader

"Matt and I met when he was my manager at Cutco, back in the 1900's! Our true partnership began eight years ago when I was returning to the workforce after having my third child, lacking confidence and battling impostor syndrome. Matt's contagious optimism and techniques for tackling challenges and opportunities have allowed me to rebuild my confidence and stay true to my core values. Our coaching sessions remind me to continue learning, leaning-in, and looking for the lesson in each experience."

— **Jessica Fincher**, Director of Sales - Ove Decors

"Matt is such a quality guy. He shows up 110% with everything that he does and is an extraordinary coach and eternal optimist."

— **Brianna Greenspan**, Growth-mindset Coach; Author; Educational Consultant

"Matt is absolutely right about how powerful it is to CHOOSE the attitude in which we move through adversity and challenge. This isn't to suggest that we stuff our feelings of shock, shame, fear, and despair. Instead, Matt's orientation is to feel those natural emotions, validate them and then let them go. When I realized

I couldn't stop drinking even when I really wanted to, I felt all of that negative stuff: shame, fear, self-doubt. What's kept me alcohol-free since 1999 is hope, envisioning and working towards a bigger future and focusing on my progress instead of how far short of perfection I am. Matt has a generous, inclusive, inviting spirit. As soon as we met, I felt an instant connection. You can count on what he says as being sincere and kind."

— **Kay Allison**, Keynote Speaker; Best-selling Author of *Juicy AF*

"It is with immense joy that I share my admiration for Matt, a cherished friend and the brilliant mind behind his first book. Matt's intentional approach to life, from his deep presence with his children and wife to his genuine connection with his own emotions, is truly inspiring. What sets Matt apart is not only his profound insight but also his remarkable sense of humor and perfectly timed sarcasm. His ability to bring laughter into any situation adds a delightful layer to life's journey. Congratulations on this milestone, Matt – your book not only reflects your wisdom and intentionality but also showcases the incredible humor that makes every moment in your presence truly special."

– **Andy Hakiel**, Front Row Dad

"I met Matt before I experienced a ton of trauma in my life. The little girl he initially met grew into a confident personal trainer, but not without crossing several hurdles beforehand. Two years ago, my husband and I were in a horrific motorcycle accident. My husband lost his leg, and I shattered my femur. Fast forward two years later and a lot of healing mentally and physically I am now facing a revision surgery on my femur. Matt's *Eternal Optimist*

Podcast has helped me grow and learn through my trauma. His thoughtful words and constant support to his clients and listeners not only helped me get over a hard season in my life, but the business perspective of his podcast has helped me grow as a leader of my gym. I've obtained the lead trainer position here and have learned how to make this business successful through passion and hard work. I truly believe Matt has found his purpose in life helping others reach their full potential all while he works on reaching his greatest potential. Practice what you preach, right? Thanks, Matt."

— **Savannah Royal**, Lead Trainer at Burn Boot Camp Carrollwood